THE TRAIN of LOST THINGS

AMMI-JOAN PAQUETTE

PHILOMEL BOOKS

PHILOMEL BOOKS
an imprint of Penguin Random House LLC
375 Hudson Street, New York, NY 10014

Library of Congress Cataloging-in-Publication Data
Names: Paquette, Ammi-Joan, author.
Title: The train of lost things / Ammi-Joan Paquette.
Description: New York, NY : Philomel Books, an imprint of Penguin Random
House LLC, [2018] | Summary: Marty goes in search of the mythical Train of
Lost Things, hoping that by finding his heart's possession he can save his father
from cancer, but he discovers that, without a driver and conductor, the train is
malfunctioning and only Marty and his new friends can fix it. | Identifiers: LCCN
2017014969 | ISBN 9781524739393 (hardcover : alk. paper) | ISBN 9781524739409
(ebook) | Subjects: | CYAC: Lost and found possessions—Fiction. | Fathers
and sons—Fiction. | Railroad trains—Fiction. | Magic—Fiction.
Classification: LCC PZ7.P2119 Tr 2018 | DDC [Fic]—dc23
LC record available at https://lccn.loc.gov/2017014969

Printed in the United States of America.
ISBN 9781524739393
1 3 5 7 9 10 8 6 4 2

Edited by Jill Santopolo.
Design by Jennifer Chung.
Text set in 11.25-point FreightText Pro.

For all those who have ever lost
something irreplaceable,
and for Kim, whose jacket
started it all

CONTENTS

1

THE JACKET (WHICH WAS THE START OF IT ALL)

The last time Marty Torphil saw his jacket, he was tucking it safely inside his mother's suitcase. It had been one of those busy-rush mornings, with Mom dashing around the hotel room checking in drawers and under beds to make sure nothing was left behind. They had planned to stay through the long weekend—business meetings for Mom, rare unlimited screen time for Marty (he was dominating at *Creature Smackdown*)—but an urgent phone call had changed all that. Back home, Dad's health had taken a sudden nosedive.

"You all packed up, Marty?" Mom asked distractedly.

"Toothbrushes . . . passports . . . heels? Where are my good heels?"

"Uh-huh," Marty said. His own bag was full, but even if it hadn't been, Marty would have wanted the jacket in Mom's suitcase. *A place for everything, and everything in its place*: Marty had read this somewhere once and had taken it as his personal motto. In this case, the jacket's place was in the safest possible spot, and that's where he put it.

Marty smoothed the dark blue denim and tucked the sleeves around carefully, protecting the twenty-six pins and patches fastened all over it. Each piece had been carefully chosen and each was set in just the right place. He didn't want any of them to get messed up or fall off if things bumped around inside the bag.

"Okay. I think we're ready," Mom said, blowing out a puff of air that mussed her bangs. It left one wisp pointing straight up like a tiny exclamation mark on top of her head. Marty wanted to reach over and smooth it back into place. "The flight's at ten, so we need to dash. You done with that jacket?"

"Almost." Marty flattened his most precious possession and tucked it safely into its place in Mom's bag. Then he put down the flap and Mom started the usual zip-and-squash routine to get her suitcase shut and to keep all the mountains of stuff inside from spilling out.

At long last they were off, bags in hand. Then it was taxi, walk, escalator, security line, planeplaneplaneplane, deplane, taxi—and finally they were turning onto their familiar tree-lined street. Sometime in the three days they'd been gone, the trees had whipped out their boldest, brightest colors. The fiery red and gold leaves flashed even in the dimming light.

As their brick house came into sight, Marty's heartbeat quickened. Dad had seemed fine when they left, barely coughing at all, gorilla-thumping his chest to show how strong he felt and waving off Mom's worries about traveling so far away. How could things have changed so fast?

It was getting dark out, but a yellow light glowed, stubbornly cheerful, from the window of the downstairs den. Marty wouldn't call it the Sick Room. He *wouldn't*.

A few minutes later, they burst through the front door in a bustle of bodies and bags and cold-snap fall air.

"It's my two favorite people!" Dad's voice calling from the den was a bit weaker than Marty remembered it, but warm and playful as always.

"Dad!" Marty yelled, dropping his bag and pushing through the heavy wooden door. Nurse Carla ruffled his hair as he blew by her, then she slipped out into the hall. She and Mom started talking in low voices.

"Scooter," Dad said.

"*Daaad*," said Marty, but he didn't really mind. Funny how much can change in four months: You can go from hating your babyish nickname to thinking it's the greatest word in the world. Swallowing hard, looking at his dad's face, all dark circles and pointy edges and long shadows, Marty forced himself not to think about everything else that had changed in the last few months.

"Sit on down," said Dad. He tried to make room, and his special hospital bed creaked on its metal frame.

Marty shook his head. "I'm good here," he said, perching on the edge of the mattress. "What about you? Nurse Carla said you were—"

Dad flapped a hand weakly, like he was brushing away Nurse Carla and her false alarm. But Marty could see from the tightening of his lips and the tensing of his jaw how much even that small gesture cost him.

"There'll be time for my health update later," Dad said. "Now I want to hear about your trip. Tell me *everything*."

These were Marty's favorite times: when Dad was well enough to sit up in bed, to talk and laugh and listen and pretty much do stuff like he'd always used to before he got sick. Just from his bed instead of his armchair. It was especially good tonight, when Marty had so much to catch him up on after their time away.

All too quick, though, their time was over. Dad's shoulders started to droop, and Mom and Nurse Carla bustled in to get him settled for the night. Nurse Carla was gentle and efficient as always, but Mom moved like a robot stuck on half speed. Her eyes were ringed in red and her hair was a scruffy tangle.

Marty edged farther and farther toward the side of the room. Finally, he felt the bump of the doorpost behind him. Nurse Carla had cranked down the lifty top of Dad's bed so he was lying flat, his eyes already closed. His hand clung to Mom's while Nurse Carla fiddled with his medicine drip.

Squeezing his hands into fists, Marty turned and bolted from the room. He ran straight for Mom's suitcase, which lay toppled over on its side in the entryway. He knelt in front of it. Then he froze. The zipper was half open. There was a tear in the tough fabric of the case. Marty yanked the bag open the rest of the way and grabbed for the corner where he'd left his most prized possession.

Where was his jacket?

Marty started to pull things out of the suitcase. He knew exactly where he'd put it. The jacket should have been right there—in that back corner—

But it wasn't.

"Mom?" Marty said. He'd been sitting on the last step of the staircase, the one that stuck out round like a bottom lip and made a spot just big enough for sitting. He'd been there so long that his behind felt like a flat tire.

Mom jumped visibly. She reached out and flicked on the light switch. "What are you doing sitting here in the dark? I thought you went to bed ages ago."

"I was waiting for you." Marty struggled to keep his voice low. He couldn't wake Dad. "I need to ask you—"

"Wait—what's all this stuff all over the floor? Did you unpack your—wait—*my* suitcase? Right here? Marty, *what's going on?*" Mom's voice went from concerned to angry to super freaked out, all in one stretch, like maybe she thought Marty had lost his marbles right there in the entryway.

Not my marbles, Marty thought. *My jacket.* Which was so much worse. He swallowed, trying to make his voice sound normal. "My jean jacket. The one Dad got me for my birthday. I put it in your bag, remember? Back in the hotel?"

"Sure," said Mom, already scrabbling at the clothes all over the floor. "You can't just throw stuff around, though. Help me pick all this up. Are you feeling okay?"

"It's not in there. I looked through the whole bag. And the zipper's all messed up. Did you move my jacket somewhere else?" Marty stood up. His legs felt like they had swarms of ants running up and down them.

"I didn't touch it, honey. Which bag did you put it in?"

"It was in this one. You *saw* me put it in." Marty was getting desperate. This couldn't be happening. He needed to be holding the jacket, needed to be wearing it *right now*. "I looked through *all* the bags. It's not anywhere, Mom. *It's gone!*"

Mom glanced up from where she squatted on the floor. In the dim hallway light she looked impossibly tired, like a display screen on its last bit of battery power. "Marty. It's getting late. I'm sorry about your jacket, but I just don't have the energy right now. Especially not with your dad and . . . everything. I'm sure we'll find it, okay? Why don't you go up to bed and we'll figure this out tomorrow."

Marty shook his head. He didn't trust himself to say anything. Not now.

A place for everything. Everything in its place. But this time it wasn't.

The jacket was gone.

2

THE RITUAL OF PRESENT OPENING

The jacket had come to Marty in the most ordinary of ways: On the night before his last birthday, Dad took him out for their traditional burger and milkshake. "Just us boys," as he liked to say. Between slurps of thick, frosty chocolate and bites of meaty, cheesy goodness, Dad had slid a box across the table. It was one of those big Priority boxes that his mom kept a stack of in her office so she didn't have to run to the post office every time she wanted to get something packed up to mail, which was super often. The box wasn't wrapped or anything, and the front flaps were tucked under each other in this complicated way that made it stay shut without tape. Dad hated crafty stuff, but he'd clearly put this together on his own.

So right away, this box sparked Marty's curiosity.

Marty was good at making connections, and here is what he could tell straight off.

- Dad had packed this box himself, without Mom's help.
- Dad was giving it to him tonight *instead* of at his birthday party tomorrow.
- Therefore, the present—well, it had to be a present, right?—was something extra special. Secret, maybe even. Something for only the two of them.

Shoving his milkshake out of the way, Marty grabbed the box in both his hands. He almost yanked it right open, but just in time he remembered their present-opening ritual.

If ever a present needed to follow the ritual, this one did.

Catching Dad's eye with a big grin, Marty hefted the box up in both hands. The box was wide but not very tall, and bigger around than his head. It was also pretty light.

"Heavier than a boiled egg," he said. The rule was you had to say the first thing you thought of that fit. "Lighter than a laptop."

"Boiled egg?" Dad laughed. "You try and find something lighter than that."

Marty laughed, too. He shook the box. "No rattle." He shook it again. "A little wiggling around in there . . . a hamster, maybe?"

Dad laughed again, then he coughed. The cough triggered a bigger cough, and Marty frowned. Dad waved a hand as if to say, *I'm fine.* But he coughed for like a whole minute, which was not normal.

He'd been doing that more lately.

"Mom would tell you to wear a sweater when you sit in the air-conditioning," Marty said when Dad finally got his breath back. He was still holding the box up and hadn't even realized his arms were starting to cramp. He lowered the present to the table.

"Sweater, *schmetter.*" Dad straightened up. His face was back to its normal color. "Get on with your gift, mister."

Marty did. He grabbed the flaps in both hands and yanked them apart. The inside of the box was stuffed with crumpled . . . tissues? He looked up at Dad, whose face was bright with held-in laughter.

"Don't give me that look," Dad panted. "They're not *used* tissues. I needed something"—he coughed again, but only once— "to keep it from sliding around in there."

Marty shook his head. *Dads.* Then he turned the box upside down on the table. Crumpled tissue blew everywhere. Even if they weren't used tissues, it was still kind of gross to have inside a present. All that disappeared, though, when the clouds of fluff parted to show a bundle of cloth. Jeans?

"A jacket," Marty said, pulling it out. "You got me a jean jacket."

"Ah!" said Dad, lifting one finger up in front of him. "It *looks* like a regular jean jacket. Doesn't it? But mark my words, Scooter, this is *far more*. This is a whole thing. A me-and-you thing. Here's how it works." With that, Dad fished in his shirt pocket and pulled out something little and round and crayon-bright. It was a metallic button the size of Marty's thumb, and it showed a picture of a fat, juicy burger on the fluffiest of buns. On the back of the button was a pin. "See?" said Dad. "This is our first collectible. Stick it on anywhere you like, Scooter."

Marty's eyes widened as he took the pin and pushed it right through the front of the jacket, below the collar. Then he put the jacket on over his T-shirt. He turned to check out his reflection in the diner window. He thought he looked ready to go on some kind of a magical quest, like the jacket was a superhero's cloak that came with its own secret powers.

"Well?" Dad said.

"I love it," said Marty. "Seriously. It's the best. And we'll get more of these things?" He stroked the pin with a fingernail.

"Tons of 'em," said Dad. "One for each memory we never

want to forget. See? That's how you capture today and keep it forever."

That was a little over four months ago, and a week hadn't passed since then without Marty adding one or two pins to the jacket, each of them linked to a particular Dad-ish activity or thing they had done together. A trip to the circus. Bumper cars. Sunday-morning pancakes. The buttons weren't that easy to find—especially not specific pictures like that—but Marty was a champion finder. He got some great ones online, and then he found this dusty old store downtown that Mom took him to sometimes, where they had a crazy selection. He'd bring each new pin back and sit on Dad's bed while they talked about the event it was linked to—*reminiscing*, Dad called it—and decided the best spot to pin it on. He'd even gotten a big patch in the shape of a dog that Dad helped him iron on to the jacket's back. That was the only collectible that wasn't linked to something specific—Marty just liked the dopey look on the dog's face. It gave him that good feeling in the pit of his stomach.

These days, he needed to catch that good feeling wherever he could.

Because the jacket was about the only good thing that had happened in the last four months. They'd had Marty's birthday party the day after the present, and it had been the best. Then the next day, Mom and Dad had sat him down together and had the Sickness Talk: Dad had cancer. The bad kind. The kind that took your body—your whole life, actually—and turned it inside out and upside down.

After that, everything started changing really fast. The doctor trips (way too many of them). The hospital stays (though Dad always came home after a couple of days). The special metal-frame bed and piles of equipment set up in the den downstairs (that was when Dad started calling it the Sick Room, which Marty hated), rows and rows of pill bottles lining the fireplace mantel, and Nurse Carla coming to help out during the days when Mom was at work.

Marty found himself changing, too. He stopped answering his friends' texts. His soccer ball got dusty. He spent most of his time in one of his online game worlds, which Mom hated but she put up with, because Marty thought maybe she got how sometimes a kid needed to lose himself inside a world he understood, a world he could control, where the only surprise that was going to change everything around was a Supersonic Vortex or a Megathonus jumping out at you from a dark corner.

Because every time Marty ventured back into the real world, he saw the changes, saw them with his own eyes. And by far the biggest change of all was in Dad himself. It didn't seem right that in less than half a year, a guy could go from being the kind of father who could pick up a nearly grown boy and toss him right up in the air, to someone who had to struggle to get a full sentence out without losing his breath.

It didn't seem right at all. None of it.

But that was just how things were.

WHEN THE WORST DAY COMES IN THE MORNING

That night they got back from Mom's business trip, Marty tossed and turned in his bed for hours. He couldn't stop thinking about his missing jacket. Kids lost stuff all the time; everybody knew that.

Marty didn't lose things, though. He always put his stuff back where it went, retraced his steps till he found what he'd dropped, and basically was the best finder ever to exist anywhere. Or that's what his buddy Jax had always said. But now there was something Marty couldn't find. And of all things, it had to be his priceless, can't-be-replaced jacket.

Did that mean it was gone forever? Could stuff really just disappear like that?

Finally, Marty got up for good, even though the too-early sky looked like old bathwater, and padded downstairs. He wouldn't have been sure it even *was* morning except he could smell the sharp brown burn of coffee on the air. When he came into the kitchen, the coffeemaker started doing that pick-me-up beeping that drove Mom nutty—she usually prided herself in catching it before the first beep; her sense of timing was that good, she said. But not today.

Mom was facing away from the machine. She was hunched nearly double, bent over the kitchen island with a cheek on the marble counter and her arms up over her head. Her shoulders were shaking.

She didn't seem to even hear the beeping.

"Mom?" Marty said, suddenly unsure. Was it too late to sneak back upstairs? His voice was barely over a whisper, but Mom's head jerked up. Her eyes were puffy and her face kind of blotchy, like maybe she hadn't slept well last night, either. And the look on her face made Marty get suddenly really, really scared. So he started talking quick, before anything weird could happen. "Did you look some more for my jacket? You know how important it is, Mom, and I looked all through—"

Mom sighed. She reached behind her and clicked off the coffeemaker, but she didn't pour herself a cup. Instead, she pulled out one of the tall stools at the counter and sat down. She patted the one next to her. "Come here," she said.

It was like there were jet packs strapped to Marty's feet, and the jet packs were trying super hard to pull him away from the room *now*. He had to force himself to stumble across the floor to the counter. He sat down on the stool, but right at the edge, his butt barely touching the farthest corner. He could feel the jet packs in his feet revving up, ready to zip him away to safety the first chance he got.

"I need to talk to you about something," Mom said.

"The jacket," said Marty.

"Something important."

"But Dad gave me—"

"Your dad is sick," Mom said, folding her lips tightly together.

Marty frowned. "I know. That's why he's got Nurse Carla. That's why we came rushing back from your meetings. Is he doing better today?"

Mom brought both hands up to cover her face. "Look, I'm no good at this. I just—you're not a little kid anymore. And I think—I think you need to know what's going on."

Marty felt like he did the first time he'd watched a horror movie at Jax's house: trapped, frozen, unable to move or even open his mouth to scream.

"You know my business trip was supposed to go into next

week. And yes, we had to rush back. Because of your dad. He's been getting sicker, but yesterday we found out his condition has gotten worse. A lot worse. The cancer has metastasized again." She shook her head. "You don't know what all that means, but the doctors are saying it's bad. Really bad."

"He's getting better," said Marty. "There's that new medicine. We're gonna ride the scenic railroad together someday, him and me."

"He's not getting better," Mom said, swallowing hard. "Marty, I've got no other way to put this. The last tests came back. It's all over, honey. Your dad's— He's— Just. There's nothing more they can do."

"Nothing more they can do?" There was a roaring in Marty's ears, or in the kitchen, or in the sky outside—somewhere something was roaring so loud, it was taking over his whole mind. The room around him started to flicker.

"Days, hon. At the most, we've got days left." Mom stretched her hand out toward him, and suddenly Marty knew that if she touched him, that was it. It would all be true, it would all be over, Dad would leave them and be gone for good. Marty yanked his hands behind him. The invisible jet packs on his feet fired up and he shot toward the door without a backward glance.

"Marty, wait!" He could hear his mom jump to her feet and call after him. "Come on, let's talk about this."

As he stamped past the door to the Sick Room, he heard shifting around inside there and knew they must have woken Dad up, too. He didn't care. It wasn't true. None of it was true.

A tornado was building inside his chest, a whirl of all his angry-sad-fear all stormed up together. Words were not enough. But words were all he had. "Leave me alone, can't you?" he yelled. "I just want to be by myself for a while!"

Clearing the last step, Marty dove into the safe zone of his room. Pressing his back flat against the closed door, he took a minute to look around. He took one gulping breath after another. Books stood in a row on the shelf, clothes hung neat and straight, everything was just right. Everything in its place.

It didn't calm him. However safe and familiar his room seemed, it wasn't. Not really—not anymore. When the very biggest and most important thing in your life is thrown out of order, how can anything feel in the right place ever again? Marty flopped onto his bed, pulled the pillow over his face, and burst into tears.

The next thing Marty knew, a hand was stroking his hair. It took a second for everything to come back to him—the rushed trip home; Mom's horrible words in the early-morning kitchen; even his lost jacket, though how could that matter anymore? He almost shoved the hand away, but then there was a low cough and his eyes flew all the way open.

"Dad?!" Marty scrabbled up, every bit of sleepiness flung from his mind. "What are you doing up here?"

Dad looked bad. Like an extra from a zombie movie, if Marty was being honest; so bad, he almost would have looked cool if it weren't *Dad*, but it was. He hadn't left his room in weeks, maybe longer. Coming all the way up to the second floor?! Marty's heart pounded so loud, he could hear it in his ears. He leaped to his feet, hastily smoothing his covers and scrunching up his pillows to make room.

"Don't you—worry—about me," said Dad. He always spoke slowly these days, often pausing to catch his breath. But now it was like the words were coming through a distortion machine. Climbing all those stairs, in his state! Dad's breath was the sharp wheeze of a saw on wood.

Marty gave Dad his arm for support and helped him settle onto the bed. He propped and fluffed the pillows till Dad gave him a thumbs-up. "Had to—get away—for a bit." He flapped his hands in front of his face. "All that—hovering! I'm—a grown man—you know. I'll catch my—breath. In a second."

The clatter of dishes rang from the kitchen, and Marty knew what that meant. "Mom's making your morning smoothie?"

"You—know it," said Dad. "But—afternoon."

Marty's eyes shot to the clock. "It's four?" He'd slept away most of the day. "Wait. Mom's not at work?" It was Saturday, but Mom's schedule was wonky these days.

Dad gave a twist of a smile, like a sad lemon. "She's taking a little—time off."

Marty concentrated on the pattern on his bedspread, noticing how the blue and yellow overlapped each other in neat, predictable ways.

"She told me—you talked."

Marty scowled. "*She* talked. I don't believe any of it. I mean, look at you. You're fine. Right? Don't you feel fine? Or *okay*, at least? I mean, you haven't been upstairs in ages."

Dad considered this as he studied Marty's cork headboard. Then (was he avoiding the question?) Dad pointed to a strip of photo booth pictures. "That friend of yours—he hasn't come around in a while. He used to be over all the time."

"Jax. Yeah." Marty shifted uncomfortably. He did not want to talk about Jax. Or his old group of friends. The truth was, he hadn't seen much of any of them since school had started this year.

They were quiet for a bit, then Dad suddenly perked up. He reached a hand into the front pocket of his ratty old sweatshirt. "I almost forgot! I got something—for you. I meant to give it to you—last night, but . . ." He rolled his eyes dramatically, and Marty let himself relax the tiniest bit. Dad's breath seemed to be coming back, too. He put out his hand to Marty, his fist clenched tightly shut.

Marty sat up straighter. There weren't many things that could be hidden inside a closed fist, even one as big as Dad's. "Is it a new pin?"

With a flourish Dad unfurled his fingers, and Marty picked up the button. "Whoa! This is incredible."

The pin was star-shaped and huge, nearly the size of his palm. It showed three little heads crowded along the bottom, and it was easy to see they were meant to be Dad, Mom, and Marty. "Hey!" Marty said. "Did you have this made specially? Is it a custom thing?"

Dad silently twinkled.

Marty went back to the pin. The tiny faces were all smiles, and above their heads swirled a gauzy sort of cloud. In the cloud was a scattering of images: a green-faced witch and a gingerbread man and a jolly red-and-white Santa. There was a long silvery train and what was clearly meant to be a dancing banana. The last one made Marty laugh out loud. "Those are all your stories, aren't they? Is this a button about our story times?"

Dad clapped his hands in delight. "Do you love it?"

"Oh, Dad." The rush of joy he felt building in his chest suddenly turned ice-cold. The button was perfect. But he no longer had the jacket to put it on. His dad's face looked so bright, so proud, so purely happy. *Days,* his mom had said. What if she was right? What if that was all the time Dad had left? How could Marty tell him the truth—that he'd taken their most special link and *lost it*? Marty swallowed. "It's the best thing ever. Seriously. Thank you so much."

They sat in silence for a few minutes. Marty ran his thumb over the button. His gaze settled on the image of the train. He hadn't thought about that story in a long time. He tapped it with his fingernail. "It's the Train of Lost Things!"

"Ah," Dad breathed out a long sigh. "That was your favorite story of all, once upon a time."

"You used to tell me it was a true story." Marty could hear the accusing note in his voice, but there was something else in there, too. Something that sounded like an odd ping of hope. That was ridiculous, right?

"I sure did," said Dad.

Marty laughed softly. When he was younger, he really had believed that story was true. He'd believed it with all his heart. But when you grew up, when you got old enough to be in the double digits, you had to leave all that believing-in-magic stuff behind.

Didn't you?

On the bed beside him, Dad looked as serious as Marty had ever seen him.

Inside Marty, something said: *What if . . . ?*

． ． ．

There are some moments that are small enough to be instantly forgotten. Blink once and they're gone, never to cross the mind again. Only later, much later, can you look back and see those moments for what they were: pivots. Enormous, life-changing crossroads where life itself hangs trembling in the balance. Then the starting shot fires and the race kicks off, catapulting everyone and everything into full motion. After that it's a blur of movement and action and adventure, but . . . look back.

It all starts from that one little moment.

That one little *what if*.

"Will you tell me the story again?" Marty swallowed hard. "Now?"

"I was hoping you'd say that." Dad patted the bed next to him, and Marty scooted close, tucking himself under Dad's bony arm. "Listen close, then. Because this kind of story—and this kind of magic—doesn't come along every day."

Dad took a deep breath, and as he started the familiar opening, his voice seemed to grow stronger with every word. "This is the story of the Train of Lost Things—and how I almost caught it."

4

THE TRAIN OF
LOST THINGS

I was just about your age the first time I heard the story of the train," Dad said.

Marty held his breath. He didn't want to miss a single word. Sunbeams slanted in through the bedroom window, filtering through the fat maple's red and yellow leaves to paint everything in the room a shiny gold.

"I had this whistle." Dad laughed a little. "Man, I loved that thing! It was all shimmery, shaped like an egg. I called it my egg-whistle. It had this goofy little rim that you put in your mouth, and when you blew on it, it made the nuttiest squeaking noise. I'd run around everywhere making the most ridiculous sounds you could imagine. I took that thing everywhere."

Marty could picture the eggwhistle in his mind. He grinned, even though he knew what came next.

Dad went on, "We were downtown one weekend—I can remember that night so clearly! It was the Fourth of July and we'd gone into the city to watch the fireworks. So it all finished up and we were packed into a crowd on our way home. Someone bumped me and I dropped the whistle. I was so upset! I looked and looked for it, but there were just too many people. We had to go home. I never saw it again."

Like my jacket, thought Marty dully. *Here one day and gone the next.*

Dad's mind was still far away. "You might think this is ridiculous for an eleven-year-old kid, but I was inconsolable at losing that whistle. My dad said it was no big deal. My mom, though, she got it. That night, she told me the story of the train."

"The Train of Lost Things." Every time Marty said those words, he got a thrill—a literal rushing thrill—all the way down to the tips of his toes. He had when he was tiny, and he did now. The name itself crackled with magic.

Dad smiled at Marty. "Yes. It's where things go when they get lost. It's a train—a magical one—and every precious thing that's lost by a child is gathered into its cars."

"What things go there?" The question came naturally, even though Marty knew the answer well.

"Every true heart's possession that is lost by a child. The train collects them all. But—"

"But?" Marty could barely breathe. It had been years since he'd heard this story. Now it felt both comfortably familiar and brand-new.

"It's secret. The train could go right by our house and we'd never even know it. Never see. It shoots across the night sky in a swirl of fog—a fog as thick as a quilt, keeping it hidden from everyone down below. But sometimes, in the very dead of night, if you listen carefully . . . you can hear the train's horn."

"Not everyone can," Marty whispered.

"Almost no one," Dad whispered back. "Only someone who has lost a heart's possession. Someone like that—well, they might. They just might."

Someone like me, Marty thought. A quiver started in his chest. "Dad, this is . . . this is only a story, right? I mean, it couldn't *really* be—" The last word wouldn't come out into the air. *True*, he wanted to finish. *Could it?* But his throat was frozen up.

Instead of answering, Dad continued his tale. Where his and

Marty's hands linked, though, Dad's trembled a little. "After my mom told me that story, I stayed up late for days. I even got an alarm clock and put it next to my bed, set it to go off every night at midnight. And then, finally, one night—I heard it."

"The horn? You *really* heard the Train of Lost Things?" Marty felt a sense of hanging suspended within a single moment, *this* moment, this story, the two of them right here, right now.

And the Train of Lost Things.

Dad nodded. "I really heard it."

They can be small, those moments where a newly born belief balances on a pin's edge of uncertainty. Which way goes the tipping point—ah, well.

That's what determines the story, isn't it?

Inside Marty, something tipped. This *was* more than a made-up adventure. "So what did you do?"

"I ran outside. I chased after it. I saw the fog and then—for the quickest of minutes, the clouds parted." His eyes closed, and when he opened them again, they glistened. "I saw it. I saw the train, sleek and gleaming in the moonlit sky. I tried to run, tried to catch up to it, but I was too slow. It was already way up on the horizon. I never reached the train. I never got on."

"And you never got your eggwhistle back." Marty felt incredibly sad all of a sudden, like the happy floaty balloon of possibility had gone *pop* and left him empty and alone.

"No," said Dad softly. His words were slowing down again, his breath returning to its usual labored state. "But I got to see it, you know? Got to see the Train of Lost Things with my own eyes. It's not the same, of course! But that did make it better. Knowing my old beloved whistle was out there. Somewhere." He grinned. "Hey. Maybe it still is."

"On the Train of Lost Things." Marty looked at the end of his bed, at the empty post where he always hung his jean jacket. He turned his eyes to the window, looking out over the quiet street. "I wonder . . ."

When the door flew open a few minutes later, to show Mom with bugging, worried eyes and a smudge of peanut butter smoothie on her chin, she found Dad sound asleep on Marty's pillows, and Marty staring transfixed out the window.

His mind was speeding in a wild, crazy loop.

The eggwhistle. The jacket. Dad's sickness. And now this.

The Train of Lost Things.

It was simple, when you thought about it: It was all connected. The Train of Lost Things gathered up the precious belongings that children had lost. You could find it if you had lost a heart's possession. That certainly described what the jacket had been for Marty. Things didn't get more precious than that.

But there was more to this whole connection. When he and Mom had gone on their trip just a few days ago, Dad was doing all right. He was sick, obviously, but the new test medicine was performing well. Marty had heard the visiting doctor say those very words. Then the call came and they had to rush home and the jacket was supposed to have come, too. This was not an ordinary jacket, no—this was a Dad-and-Marty thing, a gathered-up memory of special moments they'd shared together over the years. It was their link.

Now that link—the jacket—was gone.

And suddenly Dad was dying.

Something was broken in this picture, and Marty could see immediately what it was. It was all because of the lost jacket: That was the problem. That's when things fell apart. Everything had been okay until then—still bad, but holding steady.

With the jacket, there was hope.

If a heart's possession held enough power to bring a magical train to scoop it up from wherever it had gotten lost, wasn't it logical that this same magic could be pushed outward, too? That it could, just maybe, reach out to find other lost things—like health and wellness and being fully whole and strong again? Every time Dad touched the jacket, his eyes were brighter, his grip stronger.

All of his and Marty's shared memories were preserved in that one thing, and if Marty could get it back, could hold it in his hands, put it in Dad's hands once more, Marty knew—*he knew*—it would all be okay again.

Dad would be okay again.

Marty was a finder. He *could* find this train. He could find his jacket.

And then everything in his life would go back to its proper place. A place for everything.

Marty could fix it all.

He just had to find the Train of Lost Things.

5

THINGS YOU HEAR IN THE STREET AT NIGHT

Marty spent what was left of the day planning and waiting. (And also losing himself in *Creature Smackdown* for a bit. Which helped a lot, actually. Creatures were predictable, and once you smacked them down, they stayed down.) Dad woke up after about an hour and Mom helped him back downstairs. Then the three of them piled into the den for an early dinner. Dad fell asleep again halfway through, leaving Mom and Marty to poke quietly at their plates. Their appetites were pretty much gone by then. Dad was down for the night, so Marty crept back upstairs and Mom shut herself into her home office. She had been doing that a lot lately. He'd overheard his grandma yelling at Mom over the phone for "burying herself in her work," and Mom answered back that she had to keep busy, otherwise she'd lose it.

It seemed like all kinds of things were being lost these days.

He could have asked Mom to stay with him. He had a million questions he half wanted to ask her, but the other half of him was desperately afraid of what the actual answers might be. So he let her go.

And then he got busy. He stuffed his backpack with everything he thought he might need: a sweatshirt, an extra pair of socks, a pocket first-aid kit, and his dad's Swiss Army knife. Some rope. An old fishing kit with lures and hooks and some shriveled-up bait—because if you're being outdoorsy, why not go all the way? Then he settled himself at the top of the stairs with the iPad, where he could see down the darkening hallway and out through the cut-glass window above the front door. He cleared three brand-new levels on his game, looking up every few minutes to check the sky, waiting till the time was right.

He felt sure he would know when that was.

After Nurse Carla had come and gone from her nightly check-in, after Mom bustled out to do the dishes and her office door clicked shut behind her again, even then, Marty didn't stir from his spot at the top of the stairs. After a while he set the game aside and just waited, his gaze glued to the sky through the tiny front window. Halfway down the landing, the tall grandfather clock marked the passing seconds with its even *tick-tick-tick*, keeping him company in the dark.

Hours passed. Marty thought he would have dozed or drifted off, but he didn't. He had never felt more wide-awake in his life. In all this time, nothing changed in the sky outside. He knew what he *hoped* to hear. He wasn't entirely sure what he expected. But he didn't hear—or see—anything at all.

Finally, the clock gave one low *bong*. Midnight.

In the end, you couldn't find anything by sitting around waiting for it, could you? If there was one thing all great finders knew, it was that stuff doesn't just come for the calling. You've got to take your foot off the brake before the wheels can start to turn.

The time had come to get those wheels turning.

Creeping downstairs at last, shaking out his stiff arms and legs, Marty stashed the iPad on a shelf in the kitchen. He put a granola bar in one pocket and a juice box in the other. Then he double-tied the laces on his sneakers and tiptoed through the quiet hallway, step over step. He reached the back door. Stealthily, he pulled from his pocket the note he'd written upstairs. He'd planned to leave it in the kitchen, but he didn't want his mom to find it too soon if she came to get a late-night cup of tea or something. The back door wouldn't be touched till morning.

He read the note one last time:

Dear Mom:

Don't worry about me. I'm safe. I've just gone out on a super important mission. I won't be gone long, and don't worry, I have my phone with me. Don't call me, though. I need quiet to do what I've got to do. I'll be back by morning.

Love,

Marty

As he wedged the paper into the frame and shut the door carefully behind him, it occurred to Marty that finding this note might not actually make his mom feel a whole lot better. But he couldn't worry about that right now. He'd heard how Dad sounded when he coughed. And even if Marty didn't want to believe what his mom had said about the new results, he couldn't deny that Dad was really sick.

Marty had to find the train. He had to find his jacket, had to get it back to Dad, had to see what the magic could do. The sooner, the better.

Before leaving the house, Marty pulled the iPad back out and looked up the directions to the train station. After all, if you were looking for a train, what better place could there be to find it?

His foot was off the brake. His wheels were turning.

Now what?

The street down from Marty's house was quiet in the midnight blackness. The streetlights were making a good effort, but they barely eked out their pale orange half-moons. Still, Marty felt better under their faint light, so he made a game of rushing from one to the next, trying to spend as much time in their glow as possible.

The city at night was very different than during the day. It was early fall and the weather wasn't too cold yet, but Marty pulled his jacket tight against the damp chill. He walked for ten minutes, down one long street and up another, without seeing a single car drive by. Then he heard one coming a ways down the road, and he ducked behind a bus shelter. Somehow it didn't seem right for actual people to see him out and about at this hour. Who knew what kind of strangers might be roaming the streets late at night? Deep down, Marty knew that what he was doing was really stupid. Dangerous, even.

Or it would have been, if there hadn't been a *magical train* loose in the world. And his dad's life at stake!

How could anything be more important than that?

Marty had been to the train station a few times, when they'd gone for day trips downtown. It wasn't too far from his house. But alone, at night, it seemed a lot bigger than he remembered—kind of threatening, actually. Marty stood down below the tracks, not quite ready to go into the dark tunnel and climb the stairs to the platform. He stayed nearby, though, so he could make a quick dash for it if the train came.

When the train came. It *was* coming, right?

His dad had said there was the sound of a horn, that you knew it when you heard it. Marty didn't hear it. He waited and he ate the granola bar and drank the juice box and wished he'd brought another one of each. He kept waiting, till finally he knew that he had to be in the wrong place. Which sort of made sense, when he thought about it.

"The Train of Lost Things is magic, stupid," he muttered to himself. It felt good to hear real spoken words bouncing around in the darkness. "It doesn't need to go through a regular train station."

Then where?

He thought of the old depot. If you followed the tracks back toward the edge of town, there was a bunch of abandoned ware-houses where all the old trains used to be parked, before they got moved farther out of the city. He'd gone there with Dad once, years ago. So long that he'd been small enough to ride on Dad's shoulders to see over the top of the wire fencing. That had to be where he'd find the Train of Lost Things.

Marty squared his pack on his back and started walking again.

Following the train tracks was harder than it looked. He wasn't dumb enough to walk along the actual tracks—he'd seen this movie one time where some guy tripped and fell and got hit by a train, and Marty had never gotten that out of his mind. And for a long time there was a road that went right alongside the train's route, so it was no problem.

But after a bit he realized that the road he was on was curving away, and had been for a while. Then he heard some rowdy guys making noise up ahead and he took a side street to avoid them. And between one thing and another, Marty suddenly took a good look around himself—unfamiliar street signs, dark shuttered stores, empty parking lots—and realized—

—he was completely lost.

Marty's heart thumped in his chest. He could be *anywhere*. No one knew where he was. He fingered the phone in his pocket—he knew that if he really wanted to, he could use it to call for help.

But he wouldn't.

The bottom line was, Mom would hit the roof when she found out what he'd done. The whole point of leaving that note was that by the time he got back and had to face her anger and whatever punishment came next, he'd have already done what he set out to do. He'd have found the train.

If he called Mom now, before finding *anything*, the whole adventure would be over. There was no way he'd be sneaking out anywhere for a good long time. And time was something he didn't have right now.

No, if Marty was going to find that train, it had to be now. Tonight.

So Marty kept walking. He'd started this game level and he was going to see it through. Lost or not, he would stay out here until he found what he was searching for. Or until morning, whichever came first.

There are certain things in life—the best things, some people think—that you can never find until you are well and truly lost. Marty learned this that night. As he trudged on, pushing worry from his mind and trying not to think about what would happen next . . . suddenly, he heard it.

Cutting through the darkness like a knife of moonlit magic

came one long, low blast of a horn. The keen of a train pushing through fog. The sound of enchantment seeping into the world. Just a sliver. Just enough that, if you ran as fast as you could, you might catch it.

Run!

HOW TO CHASE AN INVISIBLE TRAIN

Marty ran.

He'd never been in this part of the city, never been outside this late at night, never felt—or *been*, really—so completely and utterly alone. He wished he'd called someone to come with him. Like Jax, maybe. He realized it was the first time in ages that he'd been able to think of Jax with something other than dread. But Jax wasn't here, and what could Marty even have said to him after all this time? Marty was on his own. He ran on.

The horn blew again, long and low.

Where was it coming from? Marty slowed, his pack thumping on his back and his shoes scuffing at the gravel. His breath rasped in the silence like the saw of wind on branches.

Or did it?

No. There was the sound of *actual* wind, too. It ruffled the trees lining the street. It gusted around him like the brush of a giant's hand, whipping his hair and furling the hem of his pants and clacking at the purple zipper pulls on his backpack.

Pinching his phone tight in his hand, Marty turned in a slow circle. "Come on, Train," he whispered. "I know you're out here somewhere. Show yourself!"

The street Marty was on was wide, with dark and dozy houses to either side. Murky streetlights fought against the gloom. Up ahead, the way curved out of sight in the shadows, but Marty thought he could make out a stretch of trees. A park, maybe? It was hard to tell, because the farther he went down the street, the thicker the fog grew up ahead.

The fog.

Marty lifted his hands, looked at the faint mist pooling around his feet. Huh. He looked back down the street behind him. The night he'd come through was as crisp and clear as ice water.

Did fog work like that? Marty was pretty sure that real, normal fog didn't get denser as you got closer to one spot. It didn't seem to be *leading* you somewhere.

He thought of his dad's words about the train: *"It shoots across the night sky in a swirl of fog."*

This had to be it.

Marty thumped on down the street. His sneakers slapped the asphalt and his breath came in little puffs. Anticipation slammed in his chest and rang in his head, almost like words: *Wait for me! Wait for me! Wait for me!*

He reached the end of the street and saw a trail curving in between some bushes. He hesitated for a second. Like ghostly fingers, the fog beckoned. And off ahead, a sound: the long, low groan of a train.

He dashed onto the path, following the narrow gravel strip till it spilled out onto a grassy field, where it kept curving across the park toward a smooth, rounded hilltop.

The wind blew stronger here in the open. Much stronger. But Marty barely noticed because the fog was billowing around him now, actual visible puffs of mist that clouded and clumped all over and through the huge open field.

The horn sounded again.

The train had to be inside the fogbank. It had to be.

For an instant Marty hesitated: creepy fog, dark night, empty park. Well, this was the reason he'd come all the way out here. Still . . .

Then something rammed him from behind and he went

flying headlong off the trail and into the grass. The wind again? No. This was way more solid—not some*thing* but some*one*.

Suddenly scared, Marty started to dive for cover in the bushes. Then he saw that the figure standing over him was no bigger than he was: wide, staring eyes in a small, shadowed face.

"Who—who are you?" came a sharp voice.

Marty jumped to his feet. "Who am I? You ran into *me*!"

It was a girl about his own age. She wore neon-orange sneakers, dark jeans, and a blue sweatshirt with the hood pulled over her head. Her hands were fisted up in a boxer's stance and she looked as steaming mad as Marty felt.

"Well?" she challenged. "What are you doing standing like a lump at the end of the path? In the middle of the night?"

"Why were *you* running crazy down the path in the middle of the night, anyway, without even looking where—"

The horn sounded again, but it was different this time.

A little sharper. A little more urgent.

Marty spun back toward the field. The fog puffed and billowed. He took a couple steps in its direction before he realized that the girl was at his side. But she wasn't paying attention to him anymore. She, too, was facing the field, staring out toward the fog.

Listening intently.

Marty turned his head, considering her. "Do you—do you hear that?"

"The horn," she said slowly, like she was testing him.

"Of a train," said Marty.

"*The* Train," she began, and Marty rushed to finish along with her, "of Lost Things."

They faced each other, eyes wide, for two or three beats. Then the girl nodded crisply. "I've got to catch that train."

"Me too."

"All right," she said. "We should do this together. Team?" She held out her hand.

Marty frowned, then nodded and gave her hand an awkward slap/shake. "Team. I'm Marty Torphil."

"Dina Khan. We're gonna have to go all the way inside the fogbank. It's got to be in there."

"Yep." Marty was pleased that they were thinking along the same lines.

Then they both hesitated, evidently each thinking the other might go first. Finally, Dina rolled her eyes. "Come on, we'll go in together. Safety in numbers and all that."

Marty took one step closer to her, so their shoulders almost touched. He realized he was death-gripping his phone, and he stuffed it back in his pocket for safekeeping.

Together, Marty and Dina marched across the grass toward the great misty unknown.

· · ·

"Hey!" Dina yelled a minute later, ducking and rubbing her head. "What did you do that for?"

"Do what?" said Marty. The wind was even wilder than before, sending his hair flapping around his head.

"You smacked me on the head!" Dina's hood had blown all the way down, and her ponytail was swatting her in the face.

Marty saw a flash behind her, something whirling end over end in the wind. A notebook? In a second it blew past them, flapping like a bird on the wing. It disappeared into the wall of fog.

"It wasn't me," he said, nudging her with his elbow. "Look!"

They both ducked as a stuffed dolphin twice the size of his head swam past them through the air, like it was being pulled by a huge magnetic force.

"Lost things!" said Dina. She had to raise her voice to be heard over the roar of the wind. "Heaps of them! They're all being pulled to the train."

Just like us, Marty thought but didn't say.

They were partway up a rounded hill now, and while the fog was pretty thick all around them, the patch covering the hill's peak looked entirely different. That cloud hovered an arm's reach away, great and gluey and pulsating. Unlike a normal mist, which seemed to fade around you when you got inside it, this one was extra thick and soupy, like someone had dripped a giant pot of chowder over everything and then walked away.

Marty and Dina picked up their pace, jogging side by side. They exchanged a sidelong glance when they hit the barrier—and it *was* a barrier, almost like running through cotton candy—but then they were through, and . . . everything was different because—because—

The train.

Was right ahead of them.

They'd found it.

TAKE A RISK, SEE WHAT HAPPENS

For some reason, Marty had been imagining an old-fashioned storybook type of train, a steam engine like the Polar Express or the Hogwarts Express with a big belching smokestack and chug-a-lug wheels. The Train of Lost Things was nothing like that. This engine was round-nosed and silvery and sleek as an eel. Long stripes of fire-engine red swept dramatically down its sides. The windows were dark and shimmering and you couldn't see a thing through them. Here inside the fogbank, Marty and Dina were cushioned from the worst of the wind, and the train stood out sharp and clear against its muddy background.

The mist had thinned into wispy branch-like tendrils that wafted up and down its sides. The great machine was a short run away, poised atop the rounded hill. But—it wasn't *on* the hill.

It was in the air.

In. The air!

Well, it *was* a magical train, after all.

The engine was humming and groaning, but the train hovered a half body's height over the hill's peak. It wasn't on a track, either, which Marty probably should have expected: Magical trains obviously could travel wherever and however they wished. This train now ruled over the park—over the entire town—from its airy throne.

It also seemed—could it be?—like the train was *waiting* for something. Marty didn't know how he could tell this, but he could.

Was it waiting for *them*?

The train's headlights cut yellow-white light into the front barrier of fog. And then . . . the lights turned, ever so slowly, swinging around to aim directly at the two of them. Marty held up a hand to shield his eyes from the twin spotlight glare.

"Come on!" Dina yelled, and only then did Marty realize that she hadn't stopped when he had. Now she had nearly reached the train.

The headlights blinked once. It felt almost like encouragement. Like an invitation.

Marty ran to catch up with Dina. His pulse pounded in his ears. This was *too* unbelievable! In front of him, the Train of Lost Things hovered, three or four feet off the ground. It was nearly close enough to touch.

"How are we going to get inside?" Marty called.

There were maybe a dozen train cars, all joined together by rubbery accordion-style connectors. At each car's end was a sleek door with a huge grayed-out window, and below each door was a jumping-off step that hung down, like on other trains Marty had seen. But since the whole train was floating, the actual step was at about his chest height. Great puffs of cloudy fog cushioned below the wheels and padded it on all sides, making the train look super mysterious—and also kind of intimidating.

"We climb up to get to the doors, I guess?" said Dina uncertainly, and Marty thought he knew how she felt. Magical trains were well and good in bedtime stories, but finding one in real life—not to mention *climbing aboard* one—was something else entirely. What if it didn't like you?

What if it *did*?

As they hesitated, a porcelain doll careened up from behind them, tumbling feet over curls on a brisk current of air. It headed straight for the window of the car where they stood. Marty's mom had a couple of those dolls, which had belonged to her grandma, and they were so delicate that she never let anyone touch them (they were "for display only"). The way this was one hurtling, it was going to shatter on impact.

Marty grabbed to save it. He missed.

The doll reached the window. And then—it sank *through* the shimmery glass and was swallowed up inside the car.

Marty was impressed. This train had game.

Dina, meanwhile, started marching at the train. She reached the door to the nearest car, grabbed the step with both hands, and did a pretty impressive pull-up. With a huff and a grunt, she hoisted herself to standing. Marty's stomach twanged uncomfortably—that step was high!—but Dina showed no sign of concern. With one hand clamped onto the holding bar, she grabbed the door handle with the other and yanked hard.

Nothing. The door was locked tight. Giving a frustrated yell, Dina squatted and jumped back to the ground.

"Come on!" she shouted over her shoulder, running toward the next door. "We need to find a way in. We'll have to try all the doors—some of them have to be open!"

The train burbled, and Marty felt a pulse of unease. He ran in the opposite direction from where Dina was rattling her next door. Shaking her head, she jumped down and kept going, while Marty pulled himself up onto his own step. By now he didn't expect the door to be unlocked, though he tried it to be sure. Nope.

There had to be a solution, if only he could find it.

He considered the door in front of him. There was no visible locking mechanism. (Not that he could have picked a lock, anyway, even if he could see it, but at least it would have been something to try.) The handle was sturdy, and the only thing he could have tried bashing it with was his phone; he didn't need to guess how that would end.

Marty threw his weight at the handle. It didn't budge.

He rammed his shoulder into the door. Not even a tremor.

The train snorted. Actually *snorted*. Was it finding this whole process entertaining? Then it burped. The burp turned into a jolt.

The train inched forward. Just one step, but it was clearly a sign of what was coming next.

"It's gonna leave!" Dina shrieked from halfway up the train. "What'll we do? Why aren't you doing anything over there?"

"I'm," Marty called out over his mounting panic, "trying"—a big gust of steam puffed out from below the train—"to think!"

The horn bellowed out two short, sharp barks: *Toot, toot!* It almost sounded like, *Let's go!* Or, *Come on!* Or even, *Outbound!* Whatever it was, Marty got the distinct sense that this was not a train that waited very long for anything—or anyone.

They either found a way on, or it was game over.

"Come on, Train," Marty whispered. "You drew us here, right? So there must be a way in."

He jumped off the stoop and scooted a few steps back. He tilted his head, studying the train cars extra carefully. There had to be some clue here, something he was missing. Part of being a good finder, after all, was being a good looker. And now something nagged at him. He watched as a line of plastic farm animals flew in formation toward the train's window. In their neat single-file row they melted through the glass, one after the other: cow, pig, goat, moose (*moose?*), chicken, rooster, sheep, dog, cat.

Marty looked again at the mysterious, glimmering panes. He wondered.

The train's horn shrieked again, three short barks this time. In Marty's head it sounded like, *All aboard!* And, *Final call!* And, *Heading out!*

"Hey! Come back here!" Marty yelled to Dina as soon as the noise died away. She didn't hear him, though. She was too busy hoisting herself up onto the next step, rattling yet another door. The girl just didn't give up!

It was no use. The locks held; the doors stayed shut.

The train bobbled again. This time, it didn't stop. It was inching forward at a snail's pace, but it was definitely in motion. The cloud billows cushioned the edges of the floating wheels and moved right along with them.

They were almost out of time.

Marty had a hunch, but it looked like this one attempt would be all he had time for. If it didn't work, his quest was finished.

The train bellowed again.

Marty cinched his backpack tighter and tucked in his arms to his sides. He ran straight toward the suspended train step. From the corner of his eye he saw that Dina had turned to stare at him. Then she jumped down from her step and started to run alongside the train in his direction, like maybe she thought he'd lost his mind and was going to intercept his headlong dash.

He kept his eyes fixed on the door. This would be tricky to pull off. And if it didn't work—

No. He couldn't think that way.

Marty pushed himself to go even faster. He was nearly there—nearly there—*nearly there.*

Marty reached the train. He grabbed the stair with both hands and flung himself up into a leapfrog leap. He shot up. The moment his feet hit the step, he sprang into another jump. With one hand he pushed off against the door handle. The other hand he thrust out in front of him, straight *at* the silvery-gray surface of the door itself.

The glass parted like a curtain to let him in.

Still going a million miles an hour, Marty lost his balance and toppled in an ungraceful jumble of arms over legs over pretzeled-up backbone. He crashed hard against the far wall of the train.

But he was in.

He was IN!

Marty had made it onto the Train of Lost Things.

8

AND WE'RE AIRBORNE!

As soon as he recovered his wits, Marty remembered Dina. He scrambled to his feet. The train was moving, but still pretty slowly. He spun around to face the door. At that moment, two flattened hands burst through the same glass he'd come through. Dina's face came next—her eyes bugging out, her mouth a dumbstruck O. Momentum carried her into a handspring right at him. Marty dove out of her way.

At the last second she tucked herself into a midair somersault and came to land in a crouch. Then she leaped to her feet, flinging her arms out wide like a gymnast expecting a perfect score.

"WOW!" she yelled. "Was that something? That was *SOME-THING.*"

"That was something," Marty agreed.

"You had to be moving to get through, right? Like getting to Platform 9¾."

Marty grinned. "That's what I figured. You can't just jiggle the handle or *tap-a-tap-tap* and wait to get let in."

"You gotta believe," said Dina with satisfaction. "Makes sense."

"I believe," Marty said softly, and reached a hand to the wall nearest him—mostly to steady himself, but also to touch this mystical machine, this amazing engine that they had somehow managed to find and board. The wall panel was cool under his fingers, but a moment later—

He yanked his hand back.

"What?" Dina yelped.

Marty blinked at his fingers. "The metal got suddenly . . . hot?" He touched the wall again, but it was cool as ever. "Weird."

One thing was sure: There was more going on inside this train than mere machinery.

Dina glanced back the way they'd come. "Look at that!"

The door they had come in through looked as solid as ever (despite the fact that two very living kids had just sprung through its window like some kind of ghosts). But the windows were something else. Unlike the gleaming gray they appeared from outside, in here they shone clear—and not only clear but extra bright, like they had filters to make the outside view super shiny and crisp.

Of course the view, right then, was pretty much what you'd expect from a park on a foggy fall night: fields of half-wilted grass, murky trees with their colors cloaked in shades of gray, a chilly blanket thrown over the world.

Marty found it mesmerizing.

Dina came to stand next to him, then they both ducked as a large inflated pineapple careened through the door and whooshed over their heads.

After a pause, Marty asked, "Is the fog going away? It doesn't look as thick out there as it was."

"I don't know," said Dina. "It's been like this since we came in. I think these windows might be . . . special."

Windows? The whole *train* was special.

But it was true that from in here, the fog was less visible. Almost see-through, actually. Even though you could tell the fog wall was there, it didn't blot everything over like it had when they were outside. The train slid forward with a gentle rocking sway that felt strangely soothing to Marty. By now they'd nearly reached the yellow lights at the far edge of the park, and he took in for the first time how big the field was.

And . . . how *many* objects were coming at them.

Well, at the train.

He ducked again, then swung his whole body out of the way as two black-and-white china cats closed in on him. Thankfully, most of the objects were entering through the main carriage windows, not the doorway where they stood looking out.

"That is a *lot* of lost things," Marty said.

Dina nodded. "But—this isn't everything that's getting lost, is it? I mean, people lose stuff constantly."

"It's just from kids," said Marty.

"Even kids," said Dina. "Especially kids. I mean, I've had to buy six pencil sharpeners since the start of the school year. Six!"

Marty crinkled his forehead. "It's only special stuff, my dad said." He thought of Dad's eggwhistle, lost so many years ago. Had that, too, gone spiraling across the sky on a night like this one, coming to rest somewhere on this very train? "A 'heart's possession.' That's what comes to the Train of Lost Things."

"Oh," said Dina. "That makes sense, I guess."

It was a *lot* of stuff. Without even trying, Marty could see a flying Wheaties box (seriously? a Wheaties box?), a golf club, some kind of wooden puppet with strings dangling everywhere, a striped wool scarf, a huge old-fashioned iron key, and three different books. An eyeblink later, every one of those items had been sucked through the windows somewhere on the train. A whole new batch of stuff took its place.

"It's coming from other places, too, isn't it? Other towns and cities. It's not just from here."

"Has to be."

Kids all over the world were losing things, Marty realized. Important things (or important to them, at least). Most of those kids would never see their stuff again. Only those few who were lucky enough to find the Train of Lost Things. Kids like him and Dina.

Marty couldn't wait to start looking.

Dina's voice cut in on his thoughts. "So," she said conversationally, "why are you here? What heart's possession did you lose?"

It came at him out of nowhere, the sudden rush of panic. Her voice was so casual, so friendly, like this was just another question, just another search. Marty's mouth went dry and his stomach dropped to his toes. He turned his back on her and moved toward the middle of the train car. Maybe she'd think he hadn't heard? Would let the subject drop?

After less than an hour together, he already knew this was not the Dina way. "Marty?" she pressed. "You okay? Did I say something?"

To Marty's horror, he felt his eyes stinging. He couldn't do it, could not put into words this search of his and what had brought him to it. So he opened his mouth and said the first thing that popped into his head. "Nothing. I'm fine. But hey, we teamed up to get on the train, right? Well, we're on. Now don't you think we should, you know, go our own ways?"

Needing to get away from the awkward silence, Marty started for the door. But Dina caught his sleeve. "Wait! I mean. It's a big place. Shouldn't we stick together? We can, like, help each other search!"

The worst of it was that she was right. Marty knew it. He'd read enough about magical places to know that you never could tell what might be lurking around the next corner. Staying together made every bit of sense. But staying together also meant talking, and so he gently pulled his arm away. "Sorry. I need to do this on my own."

Dina seemed to consider this for a minute. Then she shrugged and moved past him toward the sliding doors that led to the next car.

As the panel snapped shut behind Dina's swinging ponytail, Marty sighed. Being on the train was exciting, but it was a little scary, too. Especially now that he was standing here all by himself. It really had been nice to have someone to share in the discoveries so far. But he'd chosen his path. Now there was nothing to do but get busy searching.

They'd come aboard at the end of the train, and Dina had

gone left, into the connecting car. Marty would start right here, with the last train car.

Turning for the first time to properly take in the main open area, what he mostly saw around him was *stuff*. There was stuff *everywhere*. The room was long and narrow, in the way of trains. A row of waist-high shelves ran down the center of the car, with more shelves along the walls. Most of these were lined with bins and cubbies and drawers. Each of the nooks and crannies was bursting with items. And that wasn't even counting the stuff spilling off the surfaces and heaped up on the floor.

"Whoa," Marty muttered. "Going for a bit of a 'Train of Lost Junk' theme here, aren't we?"

The train lurched and gave a sort of hiccup. Marty froze. Was that a normal sound for a train to make? What kind of machine *was* this, anyway?

With no answers forthcoming, he set that question aside and got busy searching. To Marty's eye—the eye of a practiced finder— it looked like things used to be set up, maybe a long time ago, used to be nicely organized. Like someone had been really on top of it and had gotten all the stuff in neat piles and stacks, but then whoever it was got tired of working and started tossing things in any-which-way.

It was seriously overwhelming.

To keep his mind busy as he searched, Marty reviewed the

things he *must* do, the things he still couldn't quite say aloud (it was hard enough inside his head):

- Find the jacket.
- Get it home to Dad.
- Get *himself* home to Dad.

It actually made him feel better to have this list running through his mind, almost like he was making some progress (even though he totally wasn't).

Find the jacket. Get it home to Dad. Get himself home to Dad.

Dad. A hard thumping filled Marty's chest. He thought of Dad's belly laugh that made everyone nearby laugh along; his ridiculously loud burp every time he would speed-drink a milkshake; the look in his eyes when he would stroke the hair off Marty's forehead sometimes late at night, when he thought Marty was asleep.

Marty started with the row of stuff nearest to him—ignoring the things on the floor, for now, and beginning with the bins. When he reached the end of the row, he started on the next: pulling stuff out, shifting, checking (not finding), tossing, returning.

Ugh. This was going to take a while.

Then a jolt shook the carriage floor. There was a loud grumble, like the sound of a huge beast clearing its throat. Once again, Marty wondered about the train. There was undoubtedly something extra magical about it, even more than you'd expect from a flying train (and that was saying something). Almost like . . . an awareness?

That was ridiculous. Marty swatted the thought away. Then there was a lurch in the machinery. The train began to pick up speed.

Steadying himself on the side wall, Marty peered out the window (dodging twice to avoid incoming objects). The grassy field was still an easy drop below. Then . . . it blurred.

Suddenly, they were going a *lot* faster, like one of those old sci-fi shows where the spaceship suddenly shifts to warp speed or something.

Marty felt his chest seize. He'd expected this—right? It's not like he'd thought the train would sit around all easy-breezy while he did his search. Still. Knowing something in your head is one thing, and having it actually happen to you is quite another. Especially when the *something* is a magical train and the *having-it-happen* is whisking your very ordinary, normal-till-now self into the sky in the middle of the night, heading for who-knows-where.

The churning got higher and fiercer as the train gathered speed. The lost stuff started pelting in double-quick, too—whooshing through the main windows as well as the doorway—like it was rushing to get on before the train was out of reach. Some of the incoming items had a wild spin on their landings.

Outside the window, the ground wobbled as they sped up

even more. A block of apartment buildings loomed ahead. What now? Surely they weren't going to go *through* the buildings?

As Marty thought this, the world outside jerked, then went all tilty. There were bars with hanging straps in a few spots throughout the car. Marty flung himself at the nearest one and held on tight. All around him, inside the car, stuff shifted and slid. A yellow ball toppled from a bin and went rolling across the floor. The world outside the glass was skewed, like everything in the real world had tipped over sideways. They were legitimately airborne.

The world bent.

The Train of Lost Things shot up toward the black night sky.

Soon the city block was a dot-to-dot collection of yellow lights winking way down below.

Marty wondered if some kid, waking up to glance out her bedroom window just then, might have seen the train whisk off into the sky—if she might have seen, too, a pair of round, scared eyes peering back at her from the next-to-last train car.

He wondered where they were going.

He wondered how he was going to get back home.

He figured he was about to find out.

9

THE MOVIE IN THE KITE

For long minutes Marty stayed glued to the window, clinging to his pull strap and forgetting everything else as he drank in the night view as it blew by. It was like watching a movie on one of those big IMAX screens, where they always put in an extra speed scene, sliding down a mountain or flying through the air, just so you could get that spinny roller-coaster churning in the pit of your stomach. Except this time, it wasn't Marty but the outside world that was toppling and twirling around beyond the windows.

It didn't make him feel any less queasy.

Wisps of fog tangled and twined up the sides of the train in gooey tentacles that blurred against the windows and oozed up the edges. Then—oh, no! The train was twisting sideways! Marty dropped his strap and grabbed a nearby post, wrapping both arms around it in an awkward sort of hug (secretly glad Dina wasn't here to see his wobbly panic). The loose objects started sliding and toppling everywhere, but Marty found he could keep a basic sort of balance. Whether it was the speed or the torque or some other, unknown train magic, he held his spot while the world gyrated outside. His feet felt rooted to the floor (ceiling?), but he didn't dare wiggle even his smallest toe. He didn't want to risk upsetting whatever fragile balance kept him in place.

The lost things rattled around him like popcorn in a popcorn maker.

They continued turning. The train was going *upside down*!

In spite of the lingering knot of panic, Marty couldn't keep from smiling. "Now, that's just showing off," he said, not even caring that he was having a one-way conversation with a train. If you're going to go on a magical ride, it might as well be one to remember.

This was that, and then some!

The train finished its turn, then leveled off. The landscape below settled back down straight and flat again, a crazy quilt of patchwork houses stitched up with a yellow web of streetlights.

"Wow," Marty breathed. And he could have sworn he felt, under his feet, the faintest wobble—like a reply, almost, like a pleased little nod.

What next? The car was way messier than it had been a few minutes ago. How was Marty going to find anything in this sea of clutter? The shelf he'd been searching was completely scrambled—half the stuff that used to be on was now off, and new stuff had toppled up to fill its place. He'd pretty much have to start from scratch.

With a groan, he moved back to work. Then he felt a little thump on his shoulder. He twisted around. A kite had blown in the window and snagged on his sweatshirt. He grabbed the edge and gently tugged it free.

Holding it out in front of him, Marty could see the kite was homemade—thin onionskin paper and fine balsa wood with snug, trim knots tying it all together. The designs on both sides were clearly hand drawn.

That was as much as he had a chance to think before a strange sort of pinhole blinked open, right in the center of the kite. It was—wait, was he hallucinating? Marty didn't think so—yep, it definitely was a tiny glowing spot of light, *coming from the kite*! As he watched, the edges of the light fuzzed. The pinhole whizzed open and a bright image flashed up, like an online game leaping off the screen and into the real world.

Marty blinked.

He saw two people—an old lady and a little kid—sitting at a long, rough-looking wooden table. The table was scattered with thin strips of wood and sheets of paper and fat markers and all sorts of craft supplies. The lady had a scruffy head of white hair. She was holding a slender wooden frame, tying knots around the joints to make an X shape. The chubby little kid sitting next to her was gripping a blue Sharpie and scratching a design onto stiff card-stock.

"Nana," the kid said, "look what I did! Is this good enough to go on the front side? Will it last, Nana? Nana, when will we be done? Can we go outside and fly it after lunch? Nana, what are you doing?"

The old lady didn't say something gruff or even roll her eyes at the kid's super-annoying question-attack. Instead, she stopped her knot-tying for a second and mussed up the little guy's hair so that now it looked every bit as scruffy as hers.

"All in good time, my little monster," she said, and every word was like a hug.

The kid grinned and drew a blue heart on his paper.

Marty blinked as the movie-cloud puffed away and the pinhole shrank back to nothing. The kite was a silent object once again, just like any old handmade kite. But Marty had seen that exchange. He'd watched it happen, had peeked inside that cozy kitchen for those few minutes. He turned the kite over in his hands. There it was: on the front side, two clumsily drawn stick figures who looked like they were playing Twister but were probably little-kid-hugging, with a big blue heart wrapped around their heads. He had a pretty good idea whose heart's possession this kite was.

Marty had seen a little movie in midair. But the movie was real.

He'd seen a memory carried inside this kite.

Now Marty was excited. He set the kite down on the floor at the center of the car, near a twisty metal staircase that led up to the roof. He turned back to the shelf nearest him. He grabbed the first thing he saw—an old-looking photo in a chipped wooden frame. The picture looked yellowy and faded, and showed two girls about his age holding hands, with a sunset in the background. He realized what a boring object it was and went to put it back down; only then, that pinhole thing popped up again and Marty couldn't turn away.

He watched the picture's secret story unfold.

The scene was a restaurant—loud and bustling, with people seated at cloth-covered tables calling out joyful exclamations. In the room's very center was a redbrick oven glowing with hot flames. A guy in a stained apron shoved a giant metal spatula inside and pulled out a steaming pepperoni pizza, which was whisked off immediately to one of the tables. At the far edge of the room was a balcony, and in front of the balcony were the two girls from the picture, standing next to a lady who wore a guitar around her neck on a rainbow-colored strap. The lady strummed the guitar one last time and the girls gave little curtsies and a whole bunch of people started clapping and cheering.

Then an old woman got up and said, "A photo! Let me take a photo of the beautiful and talented sisters!" She nudged the girls over to the window, and Marty could see the restaurant was on the slope of a tall, wooded mountain. The sky was pink and orange.

"Sunset on Mount Vesuvius!" called a voice in the crowd.

In the sunset's glow, a camera's shutter clicked loudly and there was a white-bright strobe of light.

This time, the jolt of the closing image left Marty's ears ringing a bit. It had been so *loud* in that restaurant! He thought Mount Vesuvius might be somewhere in Italy—had this picture flown all that way? It looked like it had been here in the train for a while. He set it down carefully.

His gaze swept across the train car. So! Much! Stuff!

Every item in this room had a story, just like the two he'd seen. Every item was precious to some kid out there, someone who was waiting and wishing and missing. And the stuff just kept pouring in. The mess probably made the space look more full than it really was. But the thought of searching this whole car, this whole train, to find his one precious jacket suddenly felt like an impossible task.

Marty pictured himself, zoomed his mind's eye all the way out to the dark night sky and the long sleek comet of a train cutting through it, and inside the Where's Waldo clutter of that enormous train, one boy. Not big or tall or strong.

Why had he wanted to do this alone, again?

His gaze drifted back to the stair-ladder at the center of the car. Tilting his head, he followed it right up to the roof. He actually felt his eyes bug out a little. The ceiling was a giant window, running like a fat ribbon down the whole top center of the train! And marching across that skylight top? A pair of familiar neon-orange sneakers.

Dina was walking along the roof of the train.

What was Dina doing up on a moving train? Loneliness and curiosity and a bit of shame, too (his cheeks burned as he remembered how he'd blown Dina off, pretty rudely, actually), tussled inside him.

Marty thought about how upset he'd been when he'd found out he lost his jacket, and when he'd first heard the news about his dad. He remembered what he'd yelled at his mom: *"Leave me alone! I just want to be by myself."* He'd kind of meant it—but he kind of hadn't. He'd needed some time to sort things out on his own. But he'd also needed to feel he wasn't alone.

Right now, he could use a friend to stand next to.

Had he totally blown his chance with Dina? There was one way to find out.

Marty made a beeline for the staircase. Grabbing the knobby metal railing, he started the corkscrew climb up to the top of the train. There were a whole lot of things right now he couldn't do a thing about.

This was not one of them.

He had tons more searching to do—he'd barely begun, in fact. But Dina was right: Things were better together.

Plus, the chance to walk along the roof of a magical train? Epic.

10

BACKSTORY SWAP

I t was a weird feeling, hiking up a tiny curlicue staircase on a moving mystery train. The steps were so narrow that Marty almost had to take them sideways. The whole thing was a bit like watching—no, like *being*—a fizzy bubble zooming up the inside of a bottle. Like he said, *weird*. With an extra dose of super weird on the side. Especially because he got to the top faster than he expected, and before he knew it his head and shoulders had oozed right through the opening window hatch, and then he was half in and half out of the train, and for a second his eyes blurred over because it was *literally* the craziest thing he had ever experienced.

He pulled himself out of the stairwell and scrambled to his feet.

The first thing he felt was the rush of dark night wind, meeting and wrapping him in an icy bear hug. Everything up here was blur and motion, reminding him how fast the train was going.

In midair. *In the sky.*

Um.

Marty made himself stop thinking about that.

Excitement. Focus on the excitement.

The second thing he noticed was that the floor was sticky. Not I-spilled-my-soda sticky, but more walking-through-sludgy-mud sticky. The surface seemed to be super-thick, silvery glass—what had looked like a window from inside the train. Peering down now, he could sort of make out the inner train compartment. Not that clearly, though; it was all blurred and shadowy in there. (Probably just as well, since you were more likely to want to look up at the sky from the inside than back down in at the heaping piles of junk.)

The stickiness, though, took some getting used to. Marty had to put a little effort into lifting his leg. It took a few minutes for him to get the hang of it. But after that, it wasn't so hard. He found that if he wiggled his toes first, his whole foot popped up quick and easy.

Concentrating, he suction-stepped across the platform. A waist-high railing ran all the way around the roof. In the center was an open area, with skinny metal benches wrapped around a curved-out railing.

On one of the benches sat Dina, watching him with a big grin on her face. "Marty Torphil! You made it up to the boss level."

He'd been so busy with the whole walking-across-a-train-roof thing that he had nearly lost track of why he'd come up to begin with. *Nearly.* "Yeah," he said, trying to play it cool but feeling pretty wobbly. As if in response to his weakness, the train gave an extra wiggle and he flailed his arms.

"Don't worry," Dina said. "You can't fall off."

"What? You mean the . . . suction thing?" He lifted one foot, then the other. He was getting better at this.

"Not just that," she said. "I mean the whole edge of the train. Go on. Try and, like, punch at the air a bit. Off the railing."

Marty frowned. Cautiously, he reached an arm out over the rail. The air there felt puffy, like an extra-thick pillow. Huh.

Right then, the train lurched and made a sharp right turn. Marty lost his balance, felt his feet scudder across the platform. His whole body followed his arm and he felt himself toppling over the railing . . . losing his footing and . . .

He bounced.

He literally bounced off a puffy air current and was tossed back toward the walkway. Fully out of control, he spiraled clear across the platform and hit the *other* side of the airflow and bounced again, then went back and forth a couple more times, like an uncertain bowling ball hugging first one gutter, then the other.

On her bench in the sitting area, Dina doubled over laughing. "Oh my gosh, best thing I've seen all day!" She paused. "And that's saying something."

His face steaming hot, Marty finally managed to catch the rail and drag himself to his feet—stomping a little, hoping the train could feel it—and plopped on the bench next to her. His heart was beating way too fast. "That was not cool," he said. "I've got nothing against roller coasters, but this whole 'freefall with an uncertain ending' is not my style. Not even a bit."

"Yet here you are, sitting on the roof of a magical train." Dina grinned. "If this whole adventure isn't like a movie trailer for 'uncertain ending,' I don't know what is."

They were quiet for a bit after that.

The train felt different up here. A lot different. Even without being in freefall, the whole concept of tearing through the dark on a train's roof, with only a low guardrail and a cushion of air for protection, took some getting used to. At first Marty stayed clenched and stiff, his back pressed into the railing, eyes on the floor in front of him. As the minutes passed, his breaths slowed. Soon he was able to look up and out—and down, even!—and start taking in everything around him.

The view, for one. Whoo-ey! It was like nothing Marty had ever seen.

The fog had rolled away completely after they'd left the ground—or, wait. Had it? Because they seemed to be zooming along over, on top of, or maybe *along with* a giant puffy white cloud. It sat below the train wheels, cushioning them, so Marty couldn't see a thing directly below them. They were in the middle of the last train car, which ended in a stubby little tail behind them, while the main train body snaked off ahead in a long twist of cars: ten or twelve of them, maybe more.

It was a very long train.

And out below them spread the city: tiny box houses, dark puffs of trees, cheerful yellow-button streetlights, and bright flares of white and red and hot-pink electric signs, all zinging and zipping below them as the train zoomed past. Talk about the ultimate gaming experience!

Finally, Marty's thoughts settled enough that he could home back in on why he'd followed Dina. "I'm sorry for what I said down there," he said sheepishly. He was afraid she'd give him a blank look and then he'd feel like an idiot, or make him sweat it out some other way. But he didn't like leaving stuff unsaid.

"Yeah," said Dina. "You were kind of a jerk. But, you know, I get it. Losing a heart's possession can be like that. Can mess us up sometimes."

Marty smiled. He didn't know what else to say, and somehow that seemed okay, too. Down below them, beyond the cloud-cushions, the city streets twisted and turned. Stoplights flashed green, then red, then green again. He had no idea how high up the train was—below them, the rooftops and trees looked like projections on a massive, fluid, never-ending screen.

As they sped along, objects continued to shoot up from the houses below into the train: popping out of chimneys, spiraling from upstairs windows. A pair of pink ballet shoes came shooting out of a tree below their cloud.

"Hey—is that the downtown library there?" said Dina.

"It looks like it," said Marty. "I've never seen it from the sky before."

"There's no books coming from there. C'mon—not even one?"

"Are you kidding? Those librarians are too organized. They're not going to let even one get lost!"

Dina laughed, and Marty joined her. Then he said, "I really am sorry I ran away before. It's just—when you asked what I'm here looking for, I guess I panicked. I haven't talked to anybody about . . . It's . . ." His thoughts were a tangled ball of gunk inside his mouth. No matter how he tried, he couldn't get them to come out right. He thought about Dad, about the jacket. Instead, what came out was, "I have a—*had* a friend. My best friend since kindergarten. Jax. We did everything together. Over the summer, my dad got sick. Really sick. And I stopped talking to everybody. Jax kept texting me and wanting to come over and I just—I just couldn't."

"Saying stuff is the worst," said Dina.

"Yeah. I needed to be alone, I guess. I couldn't be with people who would ask me what was going on. Not even him. Because then I'd have to talk about it, and that would make it real, you know? More real, I guess." He shrugged. "After a while, everyone stopped talking to me and I guess even that was easier. I could just sort of be invisible."

Dina took a breath. "I get that. You don't have to tell me anything you don't want to. Seriously. Do you want me to tell you mine, though?"

Marty nodded. He *had* wondered.

Dina leaned in so that even though her voice was low, he could hear her clearly over the rushing train-top wind. "I'm on the train to find my mother."

Marty blinked. Now, that was something he hadn't expected. "Your—mother? You think she's on the train . . . you mean, in person?"

"No, not in person." Dina frowned. "I wasn't born in this country. I came over when I was like five, but—without my mom. She sent me to live here with my dad."

Marty's eyes went wide. His mom had been crazy busy since his dad had gotten sick, and honestly, between her taking care of

Dad and keeping up with her work, Marty could go days barely seeing or talking to her at all. But at least she was always around somewhere, always sort of nearby. Who would send their kid away forever?

Dina waved away his unvoiced questions. "It was complicated. She wasn't able to get into the country, so she couldn't just come and live here. But I could. She wanted me to have a better life, blah blah. So she sent me and my dad to live here, near my grandma and the rest of his family. We never saw her again."

"Wow. And your dad . . . ?"

"Oh, he's fine. My grandma, too. I love them, they love me. But—I don't know." She shrugged. "It's not the same, is it? They're not my *mom*."

Marty thought about connections. He thought about the way he could sit side by side with his dad for hours, neither of them needing to say a word. Or they could exchange a look—just raise one eyebrow—and it would make them laugh for ten minutes at a time. His mom was great, and she loved him, and he loved her, but . . . it wasn't exactly the same. Some bonds were special.

"Yeah," he whispered. "I get it."

"Anyway," Dina said. "The only thing I have from her—I mean, I'm sure she sent me with my suitcase full of little-kid stuff, clothes or whatever. But that's all long gone. The only thing I had left from her was a locket." She raised her thumb and forefinger into a round shape. "About this big. It had a little photo of my mom and me."

Marty tilted his head. Something in Dina's face said she had more to say, and sure enough, a moment later she went on.

"It's—the locket is shaped like a train. I told you I don't remember my mom, and it's true. I have almost no memories of her. One of the few things I remember is her telling me a story about a magical train. I think I only remember that because the locket always made me think of it."

"Then you lost it." Marty felt his shoulders wilt in sympathy.

Dina nodded. "When I realized the locket was missing, I guess I knew it would be here. On the Train of Lost Things. I don't remember much of her stories, but that bit stuck."

"Don't you ever hear from her?"

"Never." Dina shook her head, and something pinched in her face. Like a door slamming shut. "So you see why I had to come find it. That locket is the only thing of hers I have left. I want to have some bit of her, you know? I need to. The train is my only hope."

Marty let his gaze stretch out the length of the long, long train. "I know the feeling," he whispered.

"I'm sorry about your dad," Dina said.

Marty sat up straighter. "He's going to be okay. I mean, as long as I can find my lost object. That's why I'm here."

Dina raised a pair of tell-me-all-about-it eyebrows, and so he did. He'd gone this far, after all. It was the first time he'd put his whole story out in words, and hearing it hang in space against the night sky made it sound horribly, inescapably real. *Dad* and *cancer* and *dying* and *jacket* and *last hope*. As he neared the end of his tale, he noticed that the roar of the wind wasn't the only sound he was hearing. There was a low, strangely high-pitched hum in the background.

"What *is* that?" Dina asked.

The keening stopped suddenly, bleated once, then stopped again. And Marty knew.

"It's the train," he said.

"The horn?" said Dina. "That sounds way different than before."

"Yeah." What he didn't say was that it sounded a bit like sadness, like sorrow and sympathy all mixed up together. That would be too much, even for a way magical train.

Wouldn't it?

Dina stood, reached out a hand, and yanked Marty to his feet. "So. A jean jacket covered in pins, and a train-shaped locket. We've got a lot hanging on our search, so we'd better get started. There's a whole lot of ground to cover."

11

THE WORST MESS IS A LOST-STUFF MESS

s they scrambled back down the twisty stairs into the train car, Marty took a second to appreciate the quiet inside, away from the billowing wind up top. Then he thought of something. When he'd held those objects earlier, he'd seen images from their pasts, memories of the special moments that linked the lost things to their owners. He wondered if Dina had already discovered that trick.

"Hey, look at this!" he called, then stopped. He was sure he'd left the kite at the bottom of the stairway. "Wait—where did that kite go? I put it down right here."

Dina laughed. "Are you kidding me? Do you even see this junk pile of a room? It probably got buried in a landslide."

"I guess," said Marty. But he knew he had put the kite down right there. He'd noted it specially, because the color of the floor looked like the table in the memory clip he'd seen. Still, where else could it have gone?

He frowned. Had there been other stuff scattered along the ground next to the staircase? He thought there might have been, but he couldn't say for sure, especially after all that loop-de-loop train action earlier. This patch of floor was super bare now. *Suspiciously bare,* he thought.

Was there someone else on this train with them?

"All right," said Dina. "You take the left side of the car and I'll take the right. We'll each look for both things—my locket and your jacket. If either of us sees something that could be it, we'll show each other. Double the search power, right?"

"Right," said Marty, starting to get excited. He'd gone through some of this car already, but with all the mess, it was hard to tell what. Two people looking would go twice as fast. This could really work!

"This could really work," Dina said.

Marty met her grin and matched it.

. . .

They dove in. Marty showed Dina the memory-movie trick, and she went nuts for it. They learned that holding a lost object for more than a few seconds would activate the movie blast—but the object had to be held long enough against their skin for that to happen. Marty liked dipping into these clips (it was like watching movie trailers, only way, way better). But they soon realized it would take a lot longer if they spent all their time watching the origin stories for every single thing they touched.

"Do this," said Dina. She pulled her sleeve up over her palm and wiggled her fingers until her whole hand disappeared inside the opening. Then, using the fabric like a glove, she started sifting through a deep square box on her side of the car.

Marty nodded. He yanked his sleeves up over his hands and began sorting through the container nearest him. There was *so much stuff!* He saw beaded plastic hair clips and jeweled dog collars; charm bracelets and Matchbox cars; a pale green mesh pouch packed with a whole collection of sparkly earrings; a metal hourglass charm—small but intricate, with a moving bit so that it looked like the sand dropped through when the train jogged it from side to side.

They were going too slowly. Now that he'd gotten properly into this, Marty saw it could take even longer than he'd thought. What if their time on the train ran out before they found their stuff? How long even *was* their time on the train?

Along the sides and down the center of the car were long, low shelves, stuffed with baskets and boxes and bins. Every one of these was filled with a jumble of stuff, things in all shapes and sizes. Not to mention the objects that had rolled out and around during the train's last escapade: a brightly painted harmonica, a stuffed walrus hugging a chubby plastic cow, and a whole unbroken circle of hand-drawn paper dolls. Across the car, Dina worked like a bulldozer on full power.

Marty was thinking hard. "There has to be some kind of order to the train. Stuff wouldn't be tossed inside here totally randomly." He swallowed. "Would it?"

Dina looked at him. Then she looked at the mess. Then she looked at him again. It was the sort of deadpan stare you see in cartoons, that says, *Seriously?!* Marty groaned. This train car was 100% junk pile. There was no order.

Marty remembered his first instinct, how it felt like the train had used to be organized before it got all wild and weedy. "Doesn't it seem like the Train of Lost Things *should* be less messed up? I mean, it's a magical train. Why would something magical be such a wreck? That can't be on purpose." He paused. "I wonder if the train is working properly."

Dina whistled low. "You think the train is broken?"

"I don't know. It seems like it's driving around just fine. But if stuff keeps coming in all topsy-turvy like this—that can't be good.

Can it? I mean, look at this car—it's packed! What if the whole train gets overloaded? What happens if there's no more space for all the lost stuff to go?"

Marty thought about all the hearts' possessions here on this train, waiting for kids to find them. (Or whatever happened to the lost stuff after it got on the train.) It was hard to imagine anyone finding *anything* in this disaster.

No. Marty wouldn't let himself think like that. He couldn't.

"You're right. This can't be the way the train is supposed to be," said Dina. "Something's messed up here. Something's broken."

"But what?" Marty scuffed the nearest pile of stuff with his foot.

"Maybe we can figure it out as we go," said Dina. "Do something to help the train, too."

Turning to the nearest pile, Marty watched as a pair of bowling shoes (laces knotted and heels clacking together) came careening through the window and settled on top of the nearest drift of stuff.

Wait. On *top* of the drift. "How long ago did you lose your locket?"

Dina looked up. "I saw it was missing like a week ago. No idea how long it's actually been gone."

"Mine was the day before yesterday. But check how the stuff

is piling up here. Our missing things should be near the top of the mess, right? We just have to find out what cars they came into." He stared doubtfully as the drifts of items shifted from side to side when the train gave a jaunty wobble.

Dina shook her head, and Marty pictured her tiny locket landing in this heap of stuff—trickling into tiny drops and cracks, down and down and down. Before he could say anything, she squared her jaw and looked him right in the eye. "I'm not gonna lie—this could take ages," she said. "Like you said, the train's obviously been messed up for a while."

"But?" Marty said.

"But I think we're up for it. Don't you?"

He looked at her in silence for a few seconds. Then he felt a smile break over his face. "Yes! We *so* are."

Dina swung around and sank her arms up to the elbow in the nearest stack. "We'll go through the whole train if that's what it takes. Every car. I'm in no hurry."

Marty grinned as he tossed the bowling shoes aside. "You aren't?"

"Okay, I *am*. But you know what I mean. We keep looking, as long as we need to. We'll find our stuff sooner or later. Right?"

Deep down, Marty wasn't entirely sure he agreed. It's not that he didn't think they'd find their stuff. He really, really hoped they would. But that was the thing about being a great finder: You had to have realistic expectations. And what Marty's realistic expectations said when he looked around at the mountain of rubble and raw clutter was: *You'd be lucky if you didn't lose your own two feet in a mess like this.*

Still. They had to keep looking.

Game on.

Pretty soon, Dina and Marty had done all the searching they could do inside the carriage they were in. They'd checked every bin, box, and barrel. They'd found nothing. Dusting off his hands on his pants, Marty walked to the door that led to the next car.

He pulled on the handle. The panel hissed open, and Marty and Dina stepped into the accordion-shaped connecting tunnel. It jogged and swayed from side to side, way more wobbly than the main train cars (which suddenly seemed super smooth by comparison). Inside, the wind whistled nearly as loud as it had up on the roof. Marty felt like he'd been dropped inside a T. rex's lung. Which would have been pretty cool, if he'd had any brain space to properly enjoy it. Instead, he pushed right through to the opposite door and stepped out into the new carriage.

Barely one step in, Marty came to a short stop. He felt Dina crash lightly into his back. "Whoa!" Marty said, blinking. If the last car was cluttered, this new one was a disaster zone. Without even turning his head, he could see a shiny red ukulele, a glass bottle shaped like a bridge, an enormous gray sweater that looked hand knitted, a puffy pillow shaped like an owl . . .

And a zillion other things. All scattered across the storage space and floor alike. Scattered *everywhere.*

"Good grief," muttered Dina, who had come to stand next to him. With a shake of her head, she tucked her sleeves in tighter over her hands, slowly and with purpose.

Marty grinned at her. "You up for this, partner?"

"Super up," she said. "Let's whip this space."

They fell upon their search with gusto, digging, sifting, sorting, heaping, piling. There was something quite satisfying about going through a stack of junk: top to bottom, side to side, not missing a single thing. You have one thing—okay, in this case, *two* things—on your mind, and you can sharpen your whole world to that and shut everything else out. Marty felt like a boy-shaped lighthouse with a giant spotlight on his forehead. The beam was his super-searching power and it scoured every bit of the space with the accuracy of a laser. (He also thought that would make a cool online game.)

As he moved through the room, Marty found so many interesting things—some he couldn't help watching the memory clips for—but by the time he reached the other end of the car, he had not found either his jacket or Dina's locket. From the grim set of Dina's mouth, he could see she hadn't had any more success.

"Never mind," she said through gritted teeth. "Tons more cars to go."

And so it went on. They walked and searched and sorted and scoured. But every search left their shoulders drooping a bit lower; each new car was a great big fancy-wrapped present that you opened to find that it contained nothing at all. Less than nothing: the kind of black-hole nothing that sucked out your hope and zapped your energy. By the time they reached the end of their fourth car, Marty had realized something: It wasn't actually the searching he enjoyed, it was the *finding*. And this ridiculous imbalance—looking, looking, looking, but never actually getting to what he was after . . . well, he hated it.

It was like in each new train car, he lost his jacket all over again.

12

THE THIRD TRAINHOPPER

How much longer can we keep doing this?" Marty said, pausing in the accordion space between two cars. The weight of all this not-knowing and not-finding felt like having a cow sitting on his head.

Stopping next to him, Dina considered the question in silence. Then she shrugged. She reached up behind her head, pulled the elastic out of her hair, and smartly redid her ponytail. It was an impressive move, Marty thought, somehow showing that *now* she meant business. He was even more impressed when she followed that up with a firm "Until we find the stuff. Or get to the front of the train and run out of cars. Right?"

She was right (of course), and Marty opened his mouth to say so. What else could they do but keep going? Before the words came out, though, there was a thump over their heads. He looked up.

"Did something just fall on the roof?" Dina asked.

They were still in between the cars, so the rooftop here wasn't see-through. Dina started to say something else, but Marty grabbed her arm and put his finger to his lips. He had a feeling . . .

Sure enough, not three seconds later, in the same spot where the bump had been, there was a scuffle, then the unmistakable pitter-patter of running feet.

"Or some*one*!" said Marty.

They dashed into the train car ahead of them and ran for the twisty stairs to the roof.

"Over there!" crowed Dina, who was above Marty on the staircase. It turned out that the gummy-glass texture of the skylight exits was great for sneaking up on unsuspecting trainhoppers. Dina's enthusiasm, though, unlocked a new level of achievement. She sprang up the last few stairs in a quick bound, and Marty half wanted to remind her that she was climbing onto the roof of a magical train that was *hurtling through space*. But it didn't seem like the right time. Anyway, Dina was halfway down the car by the time he got out into the brisk night air.

For a second he was caught by the feel of the wind blowing his ears flat against his head, by the hot magic of the stars as they winked out from their black blanket, by the twisty-winding of the ground way, way below. Once again he had that feeling of being inside the greatest role-playing game ever made—and having a starring role, no less.

The feeling was strong enough to blow everything else from his mind for the shortest of seconds; enough to make him pause as he exited the trapdoor, fling himself into a pose (left hand on hip, right arm thrust into the sky, head thrown back), and call out: "Marty Torphil, Trainhopper!" Not very loud, though, and he yanked his arm back down quick. He didn't want Dina to hear.

Still, he was glad he'd done it. He thought he might always like to think of himself that way. Then he put all that aside and dashed across the car to catch up with Dina (carefully, still, staying to the center and well away from the edges; he *really* didn't want another scuddering tumble like he'd had last time).

It was pretty dark up here—the moon just coming out from behind a cloud—so he couldn't see very clearly up ahead. But he made out a darkish blob halfway across the car and heard the sound of squirming and grunting and muttering. He dashed over (as dashingly as he could on the sticky surface), only to realize that Dina had flattened herself on top of a wriggling, thrashing lump. She was barely holding it down.

"Help me out!" Dina yelped, looking over her shoulder at Marty. "You sure took long enough—what were you doing back there?"

"What are *you* doing?" asked Marty.

"The intruder! I'm holding it down!"

"Intruder?" Marty said. "Um. Isn't that actually what *we* are on this train? What if you tackled someone who's, you know, in charge?"

Dina went abruptly still and the lump under her took the chance to buck up, sending Dina toppling over onto her backside. Marty caught her and they both turned to the lump, which unfolded itself into a quite small, quite disheveled young person, with raised fists and a fierce scowling face.

Marty and Dina scooted backward.

"Easy," said Marty. "We're, uh, sorry about tackling you." He cut his eyes to Dina.

"Yeah," she muttered. "Sorry, or whatever."

"Who are you guys?" said the voice. A matted curtain of hair was scuffled down over the front of the small face, so you couldn't see any features clearly.

"Marty Torphil," said Marty.

"Dina Khan."

"How long you been on the train?"

"Just a few hours. Since it stopped in the park back there.

We've both lost a heart's possession, and we're here on the train to find them. For me it's"—Marty swallowed—"a jean jacket. It's super important. And . . ." He didn't think it was his place to spill Dina's secrets, and from Dina's glare, she agreed. "Dina's looking for something she lost, too."

"Who are *you*?" Dina's voice was a smidge less challenging, but not much. "You're too small to be in charge, so don't think I won't tackle you again."

Marty elbowed her. There was a time for fierceness, but as far as he could tell, this really wasn't it. He liked going things alone as much as the next kid (maybe more, honestly), but what if the newbie knew stuff? Stuff they could use? It was basically a rule of questing: You didn't just go beating the baggage out of everyone you ran into before you even knew what they were about. It made sense to wait and see.

The new kid shook Dina the rest of the way off and stood up straight and proud, tossing back the mop of messy hair to reveal a round elfin face. "I'm Star," she said, her mouth set in a grim scowl. "And you're wrong: I do run this place."

"You *what*?" said Dina. "You're not the conductor! You're a kid!"

Star turned and ran expertly toward the hatch leading back down to the car. "Shows how much you know." With that, she ducked into the trapdoor and scurried down inside, pausing only to call over her shoulder, "Be careful up there, you guys! A fall from that height could kill you."

Could kill you? No kidding, Marty thought. He tested the air cushion, which was firmly in place. He edged back toward the safer center anyway. "What do we do now?" he asked Dina. "Do we believe the kid's story? She does seem to know her way around."

"That doesn't mean she's the boss of the train. It doesn't even make any sense. She's, like, my cousin's age." She shook her head. "My cousin is in kindergarten."

"I don't think she's *that* young. She could be small for her age. Anyway, it's a magical train. Who knows how it runs?"

Dina narrowed her eyes. "Well, this train's a mess. If that kid's running it, then I guess I'm not surprised things are falling apart. Come on, Marty. Let's go chase her down."

"What? Why?" Marty ran to catch up with Dina, who was marching stiff-legged across the platform toward the hatch to the inside.

"Whether she's in charge or not, she definitely knows stuff. And that's what we need, right? An insider. I think I made a great starting impression. Now we've just gotta reel her in."

Marty gave a long sigh, then turned to follow Dina down the stairs into the car below.

13

WHAT IF YOUR IMAGINATION COULD FILL YOUR STOMACH?

They found Star in the car below. She seemed to be waiting for them, standing between a lamp shaped like a smiling squash (a label on its base said Sophie) and an action-figure kangaroo. Star stood so the lamp's yellow glow lit her up, from her pink polka-dot tights to her long gray sweater to the jaunty orange scarf looped around her neck. Her mouth had a faint green ring around it, but Marty didn't have the chance to wonder about that for long, because Dina came at her with question-guns firing.

"You say you run the train? Prove it. What do you know? How

did you get here? What's up with all the mess everywhere? Are you really that bad at stuff?"

For a second Star looked ready to run away again, so Marty said, quickly and super gently, "Don't go. We just want to know more about you."

Star's shoulders slumped. "Okay, okay," she said. "I'm not *exactly* in charge. But I've been here for ages. I'm trying my best. The train is . . . stubborn or something? Just . . . Somebody's gotta run things ever since . . ." She swallowed.

Marty and Dina exchanged a look.

"Since what?" Marty asked, before Dina could bark at her and muddy the mood.

Star sighed. "Since the last driver left."

"Left?" yelped Dina.

Star looked up suddenly, considering them. "Are you hungry? I'm hungry. Let's get something to eat and I'll tell you everything you need to know."

Marty thought of the granola bar he'd eaten back at the train station. It seemed like ages ago, and his stomach growled at the prospect of food. But more than anything, he really wanted to keep searching for his jacket.

"We don't have time to sit down for a story," Dina said, obviously on the same track as Marty. "We've got searching to do, stuff to find."

"Can't you tell us as we search?" he cut in.

"Nope. If you want to know what I know, you'll have to come along. I haven't eaten for hours and I'm starved."

They could have just left her, Marty supposed. But a quick glance at Dina showed that she was thinking like him: Star had information. She probably had answers to questions they didn't even know they had. And as any good finder knows, the best way to get to what you're looking for is to first make sure you know everything there is to know about your search. So they set off after Star.

Thankfully, she didn't walk far. In between the car they were in and the one up ahead was a little round cab. Star pushed expertly inside, where they found a cozy room arranged with a few sets of tables and chairs, and a couch-and-loveseat area. If there'd been a TV, Marty thought, the room would have been pretty much perfect. Not that they'd want to watch any shows right now (magical train and all that) but it would have been nice to have the option. Just in case.

On the other hand, maybe there was something even better than a TV. Marty noticed a strange contraption on the wall. It looked a bit like a microwave, but it was neon green and purple, with a snazzy lightning bolt on the front door. Star zipped right over to the keypad. She tapped at it for a bit, then pressed a START button. Less than a minute later, the machine dinged and

Star yanked open the door. She pulled out a plate containing three bright-green-frosted chocolate cupcakes.

"See?" she said proudly. "Snack time."

Marty's jaw dropped. "Did you just—? Did that—?"

Star grinned, her mouth already plastered with frosting. That explained the green lip smudges, Marty thought. He ran for the machine and got there a second before Dina. "How does it work?"

"Type in whatever you want to eat," said Star around her stuffed mouthful of cupcake. "Anything you like."

"That's it?" said Dina.

"I've found"—Star swallowed her last bite, apparently to get the words out more easily—"that it helps to think hard about what you want. Making a picture in your head works really well. I call it the Thought Machine."

"You're kidding," said Dina.

"Also, it only seems to work for stuff to eat and drink. Not just making up random things you want." Her mouth twisted. "Too bad."

Marty was already typing. He knew exactly what he wanted. BURGER, he typed, AND MILKSHAKE. In his mind he pictured that meal he had with his dad, the birthday meal, maybe the best meal of his entire life.

"It doesn't have much imagination," said Star, who had finished her first cupcake and was halfway through the second. "No fancy name-brand stuff. I tried to do a Coke once and it was gross. You've gotta stay pretty basic. But it does the trick."

The Thought Machine took longer to do Marty's order than it had Star's. Maybe it got better with practice? Green-frosted cupcakes seemed to be her thing. After two or three minutes, the machine dinged. Holding his breath, Marty yanked at the lightning-bolt door handle. Inside was a round white plate. On the plate was a steaming burger inside a fluffy white bun. Golden cheese oozed around a crispy meat patty, and a splash of red ketchup dotted one edge. It even looked like his lettuce-but-no-tomato order had come through. Next to the plate was a yellow paper cup holding a frothy chocolate milkshake.

Marty pulled his food out and walked to sit next to Star at the table, while Dina started pecking away behind him. His hands were shaking as though they, too, remembered the last time he'd had this meal. With Star watching curiously, he took a bite of the burger. He chewed. He thought. Then he smiled. "Not bad. Not bad at all."

It wasn't the birthday burger, not exactly. But it was close enough.

He dug in with relish, and after Dina sat down holding some

kind of wrap stuffed with way too many vegetables for Marty's liking, the three of them spent the next few minutes eating in silence. It was a good sort of silence, offset by the pleasant hum of filling bellies.

After a few minutes, Star pushed her empty plate away. While they continued to eat, she told them her story.

STAR SPILLS HER SECRETS (SOME OF THEM)

I first saw the train in the wintertime, when I was out on the street late one night. The night was cold, and I was cold, and everything looked pretty bad."

"The winter? That was ages ago," said Dina.

Star nodded. "That's what I said, isn't it? I guess you might as well know: I've got no home. Not out there."

"You ran away from home?" Marty asked.

"Nah. I just don't got one. Not for a long time. No matter why, it's ancient news, not important. But that night . . . well, I was cold, like I said. *Really* cold. It got me thinking about being warm, and places I've been warm, and with one thing and another I was thinking about my old home. Way back when I was little."

"Wait. You live alone on the street?" said Dina, sounding shocked.

Star's eyes hardened. "I'm tougher'n I look. And I'm not alone, not exactly. There's a whole pack of us. We look out for each other. Stay out of sight together."

She shook herself, like waking out of a little trance. "But none of that's important. Not anymore. Don't you see? I lost my home a long time ago, and mostly I was used to being on the street. I got by. That night, though . . . well, I started thinking. Getting a bit soggy in the eyelids. And then—"

Marty caught her shy smile and felt it stretch tight between them. "You heard the horn."

"Heard the horn, saw the fog . . . I had no idea what any of it was, obviously. But what else did I have to do with my night? I started following that sound. Like, I couldn't get it out of my head, right?" She broke off suddenly and frowned. Marty had the strangest impression she was trying to remember something. Then she shook her head and sighed. "Anyway, that's it. I heard the train, I followed it, I got on. It's the Train of Lost Things—I figured that out pretty quick. And as soon as I got here, I knew I'd found exactly what I'd lost. Different, but here it was."

"Huh?" said Dina.

"My home," said Star impatiently. She jumped up and slid her empty plate into a wide slot right under the Thought Machine. "I've come home, don't you see? Anyway, that's it for that. What *you* want to know is how to find your lost stuff, right? Basically, there are three ways for the missing things to get returned to their owners."

"Three ways?" said Marty.

Star ignored him, moving with purpose toward the door. "Time's passing, you know," she said, as though she weren't the one who had called this whole snack break to begin with. "Why don't we get busy searching? I'll tell you more as we go."

"About time," muttered Dina. But she kept right to Star's side.

Young or not, this girl had answers. Marty didn't plan to let her out of his sight for a single moment.

They backtracked to the car where Marty and Dina had left off their searching. Outside the window, fat branches of fog tapped and pushed against the pane as though hoping to be let in, but inside, the train was snug and cozy. They settled on the same sides they'd taken before and began rummaging through the bins of stuff. Marty's eyes and hands were in full-on searching mode, but his attention was on Star as she continued her story.

"So. Here's what you wanna know. The train stops once a night, right at midnight. If a kid has lost a heart's possession and hears the horn—well, you both know what happens. I don't know why only some kids hear the train and can follow and find it. Maybe they just . . . want it more? Are more open to magic? Believe? It's pretty rare, honestly. One, maybe two kids get on every week or so. Some weeks, no one at all. But that's one way you can get your lost object back, long as you find it in time." She scanned the shelves and puffed out air.

Marty cocked his head. "In time?"

"Never mind that. We're doing the three ways right now," said Star, wagging a finger. She seemed to be enjoying this instruction thing a bit too much, Marty thought.

"So what other ways, then?" asked Dina.

"The train is supposed to have two people on board to run things: a driver and a conductor. The driver keeps the train going— heading the right way, passing all the right spots so the stuff can be picked up, and keeping the ride smooth." She ground her teeth a little as she said this. Marty had an idea of how the train was doing at *that*. "The conductor is the one who organizes all the stuff that comes in. Keeps the train from getting overrun by the mess."

Dina flicked her gaze from side to side.

"Yeah," said Star. "The thing is, the conductor's been gone for ages."

"Gone?" Dina breathed.

"I don't know for how long. But, I mean, you can see how the place is."

"So it *did* used to be organized." Marty felt triumphant. If there was one thing he had an eye for, it was order and structure. *A place for everything, and everything in its place,* he thought, wincing.

Star nodded. "The last driver taught me a bunch before she left. There used to be a whole system, but the driver couldn't keep up both jobs without a conductor, so it's a total jumble now. That's why it's so cluttered in here. The stuff's not getting returned."

"Returned?" Marty said.

"That's the second way things go back to their owners. You've seen the Echo pops?"

"Echo what?" said Dina blankly, but Marty perked right up.

"You mean those little memory-movie-trailer thingies!"

"Yup." Star lowered her voice confidentially. "That's not their real name, Echo pops. If they've got a proper name, I don't know it. But I like naming stuff, and it works, right? It's showing a picture-echo of what makes it a heart's possession."

"And it pops you in the face, right. We get it." Dina nodded encouragingly. "Keep going. What were you saying about them, then?"

"Well, when you're the conductor, you're synced up with the train, like in your head or something? Some kind of magical Wi-Fi connection, I don't know. Anyway, she—or he, I guess, if it was a dude—activates the Echo so it shows all the way through. But then she can focus her thoughts on the object's owner, the one whose heart's possession it is. And, poof! The thing is sucked back out of the train and returned."

Dina's eyes were wide and bright. "Then your lost object turns up in some random spot, a place you know you looked before but suddenly, there it is!"

"Brilliant," Marty whispered. "But only a conductor can do that? The sending-back part, I mean."

Star nodded. "Unless kids make it directly onto the train. Like you two did. Then you do the searching and claim your own object yourself. Back to method one." She paused. "Or—" Star cut off abruptly.

"Or?" said Marty.

"Spit it out already," said Dina. "You said there's a third way lost stuff can get sent back."

Star shook her head firmly. "Not yet. It's gotta be done right . . . I can't just . . ." She stomped away.

Over the next half hour, Marty and Dina tried everything to tease out the information from Star, but she wouldn't say another word. Finally, they gave up in frustration and kept working through the rest of their car. Glancing over at Dina, Marty noticed that her face was getting redder and redder. He wondered if his looked the same. They scoured every box and basket, giving extra care to any piles of clothing or mounds of tiny jewelry-type stuff. He didn't want to miss anything, especially the locket, which was obviously super easily missable. But they reached the end of the car with nothing to show but disappointment. He'd actually found three separate lockets across the car, but while his excitement spiked each time, not one of them was Dina's. They didn't find a single jacket. (What, did no other kid have a jacket for a heart's possession?)

They left the car with Dina's shoulders sagging.

"Don't worry," Marty told her, trying to put a good face on things. "Remember how much stuff there is jumbled all across the whole train. We've got a bunch more cars to search. We'll find it."

Dina sniffed. "Six cars left," she said. "But you're right. And we'll find your jacket, too. They're probably scrunched up together in, like, the last place we look or something."

"It always is in the last place you look, isn't it?" quipped Star. "Funny how that works."

Not so very funny, given the circumstance. Still, Marty forced himself to keep hoping. To keep believing. The jacket had to be here. He had to find it. He *had* to!

Dad was counting on him—even if he didn't know it yet—and Marty would *not* let him down.

15

GLOWING EYES IN THE MIST

While Marty and Dina kept searching the cars for their lost objects, Star was busy with some unknown activity of her own. After she'd finished her story she'd walked away from them, but had only gone as far as the window. She'd stayed there staring fixedly, totally zoned out. Now they were in the next car and she'd parked herself in front of the window again, with the same odd staring gaze. Outside, the dark night sky blew by, with occasional pinpricks of starlight breaking up the gloom.

"Hey," Marty whispered to Dina. "Should we, um, do something about Star? She looks kind of weird to me. Does she look weird to you?"

As they watched, Star swayed from side to side. Well, the train swayed, but Star bobbed right along in time with it. She looked like she'd had a bad tangle with a cartoon hypnotist.

"Weird*er*?" Dina quipped. But she shook her head. "Let's just watch for a sec. I wonder what she's . . ."

What *was* she doing? Abruptly, Star snapped out of her trance. She took a couple steps forward, pushing past some rubble on the floor till she stood directly in front of the window. She lifted her hands and placed her flat palms against the glass.

"Uhhh," said Dina, but under her breath, so even Marty could barely hear her.

"Star?" Marty tried.

"C'mere," Star called softly. Her mouth barely moved and her gaze stayed fixed on the window.

Marty and Dina exchanged a glance. They inched toward Star.

Outside the glass, heavy strands of fog curled up and around the sides of the train.

"Did you notice earlier?" Marty muttered to Dina. "The fog was doing this same thing. Going all stringy, almost like it was knocking to get in or something?" If that sounded weird (which, honestly, how could it not?), Dina didn't mention it. Moving together, they came to stand on either side of Star.

The younger girl leaned in to the window, so close that her breath left a round frosty smudge on the glass in front of her. "Look," she breathed, then beckoned them in closer.

"What are we looking for?" Dina asked. Her tone zinged with excitement.

Marty felt the same way. He leaned in till his nose bumped the window. Was something going on outside? Star seemed more in awe than afraid. Marty squinted at the darkness, trying to look past all the fog. He didn't see a thing.

Except . . .

"The mist?" Marty said.

"The mist!" Star said. "*Look.*"

Marty looked. The outer wall of fog was thick and soupy outside the window. But what about those wispy tendrils he kept seeing on the edges of his sight, the ones that licked up the train's side and then whirled away? He stared at the nearest one. And suddenly, it was like a filter flipped in his mind. From one eyeblink to the next, the lick of mist wasn't mist at all. It had a face, arms, a body.

It looked right at him—

Marty shrieked and toppled backward. "*What*?!" he croaked.

At his feet, he now saw, a red racecar was flashing like it was lit up from the inside (though it clearly wasn't a light-up toy). On. Off. On. Off. This was far from the most unusual thing that had happened tonight—or even in the last five minutes—but Marty couldn't break his gaze from the toy.

"Give it here," said Star, in the same soft voice.

Marty jumped. "This? The car?"

"Uh-huh."

Staring at the car kept him from thinking about what he'd just seen outside the window. What *had* he just seen outside the window? Marty grabbed the car and stood up. He handed it to Star. He could tell by Dina's bugged-out eyes that she'd seen the— the *thing*—in the fog outside the window now, too. Her chin wobbled slightly, but she didn't move a muscle.

Star held the racecar in both hands. She brought it right up till it nearly touched the window's surface. Around Star's neck, every visible strand on her orange scarf stood out stiff with electric energy. Marty forced himself to look back out through the glass.

The second time, without the shock of a suddenly appearing face (or maybe he was getting better at seeing magical stuff?), the mist creature wasn't nearly as scary. In fact, it was hardly scary at all. It was a little boy. Okay, a *ghostly* little boy, almost totally see-through. He didn't seem to be more than five years old. He looked scared and unsure, and Marty could actually see fat spectral tears splashing down his cheeks.

"Hey, you're all right." Marty didn't realize he'd spoken out loud until the words were in the air. But the little guy was so upset!

On the other side of the glass, the shimmery eyes turned to fix on Marty. A thrill went through him. The ghost-boy rubbed a fist across his eyes and gave a weak smile.

"Here," said Star, and the ghost turned back to her. She held up the car. "Looking for something?"

Like a rainbow bursting through a cloud, the boy's face flashed from misery to giddy joy. He shot forward and his chubby little hands punched right through the window. Inside the train, his hands looked as firm and real as Star's own. She put the toy in them, closing his fingers tight around it. Then he yanked his hands back out, racer and all. He hugged it tight to his chest. He started to float up and away.

"Safe travels," Star whispered.

Marty kept his eyes on the little ghost until he blew out of their line of sight.

Star turned back to Dina and Marty. "And that," she said, wiping her hands on her skirt with a satisfied smile, "is the third way lost stuff gets returned."

"Okay, now. Go again from the beginning," said Dina. After the excitement had faded, the three of them had moved on to the next car and had renewed their search with fervor. Star was even helping them look. But Marty couldn't stop thinking about what they'd just seen. "This third way of getting stuff back to people. It's like the Lost and Found Department, ghost style?"

Star shrugged. "I told you that kids can find the train, living kids like us. But like I said, it's kind of rare. One or two kids at a time, maybe a couple of times a week. Ideally you've got the conductor managing some of the things and shuttling them back out to their owners. But . . . well. You see how much stuff there is. Heaps of it, mountains! Especially now, when there's no conductor. I guess even when there is one, it piles up a bit. So when something doesn't get returned, when someone dies with a heart's possession still on the train, well . . ."

"So that kid was legitimately *dead*?" Marty said, still a little stunned by the whole encounter. A magical flying train was one thing. But *ghosts*? Entirely another.

"Yup. Just another stop on the way home. The Other Side. Whatever."

"Huh," said Marty.

Dina frowned at the nearest window. "So that fog. Is it all, er, made of . . . ?"

"Nah," said Star. "It's not all ghosts. They just like to travel inside it."

"Camouflage," said Marty, who knew a thing or two about hiding in plain sight.

"Yup," said Star. "They're actually pretty shy, from what I've seen. Most of 'em, anyway. They like to hide in the mist. Usually you can't see them until they want to be seen. Or till they're super close or something. You can tell when there's one around because an object starts flashing. *Their* object."

"Like the racecar!" said Dina.

"Like the racecar. Then you've gotta find the right bit of fog where it's hiding out, give it the ol' stare-down till it pops into being visible. Well, you saw. They don't usually come all the way inside the train."

"But they can get their lost stuff back," said Marty. "That's kind of awesome that you can do that for them." Then something clicked in his brain. "You've been in the end cars tonight, haven't you? Did you move a handmade kite earlier? And some other stuff piled up by the ladder?"

Star's tiny smile was answer enough.

"I knew it!" said Marty. "I knew I'd put that down there." It gave him a little boost, to be right about this small thing. Made him feel that somehow this whole adventure was a tiny bit more under control. So much of confidence was expectation, things doing what they were supposed to do when they were supposed to do them. He hadn't had nearly enough of that in his life these days. He looked at Star's face, and he could tell that she was going through the exact opposite range of emotions.

"It's just," Star said, "I wish I could do more. It's *so* hard for me to do even one of those returns. It's weirdly tiring. Like right now, all I want is a huge nap." She frowned. "And I *hate* naps. The conductor would be more on top of it all. But I'm not the conductor. Don't you see?" Her brows were pinched and her mouth tight with frustration. "I'm *here*, but I can hardly do *anything*! I can barely help the train at all. Every day the piles get worse, there's less spirits coming by to get stuff, and the train goes a little wilder. And . . . well. This might sound crazy to you guys."

Dina snorted. "Unlikely."

"Fair enough. Okay, so the train is a machine, obviously. But it's almost like it's got its own mind or something? From what I can tell, part of being the conductor—or the driver, I guess—is being able to tell the train what to do. Getting it to make the right stops, having the incoming lost stuff go to the right places, the return stuff going out properly, that kind of thing. Basically keeping the train doing what it's supposed to do, making it behave. That's the way it's *supposed* to work: Tell it what to do and have it listen to you."

Marty remembered the thought he'd had earlier, wondering if the train might be more than a regular machine. He'd thought it was ridiculous at the time. Now? Not so much. "Like a horse and its rider," he said.

"Exactly!"

"You said you're not the conductor," Dina said slowly. "Are you the driver, then?"

Star gave the tiniest shake of her head.

Marty frowned. "So the train is like a giant wild horse—or maybe like a dragon, a silvery ice dragon. It's used to having a couple of riders in charge, telling it what to do and how to do it. But now it's on its own. No conductor. No driver. And so it's running amok."

As if in answer, the train lurched into a lopsided tailspin, corkscrewing through the air and tossing stuff every which way. Marty hunkered down and held on.

Finally, Star shouted, "Enough! You need to *behave!*"

At first, her outburst didn't seem to have any effect; the barrel ride continued uninterrupted. But a few minutes later, the train let out a disdainful sort of hiss and leveled out. The ride went smoother after that.

Star sighed. "So, yeah. Lately it's been getting harder. It's like it knows I'm not actually in charge, you know? I'm trying to do what I can, but . . ." Star swallowed. "When the driver left, that's when things started getting a lot worse. The train was mostly okay before. A bit messy, but she kept it in line."

"Why did the driver go?" asked Dina.

"I don't know," Star said. "She was here for years and years, but it was her time to move on, I guess. She wished she could stay longer, but there was somebody else ready, she said, and I'd find out when the time was right." Star sighed long and deep. "It's good having you guys here. For a bit, anyway."

When Star looked up, Marty was shocked to see her eyes were teary.

"If things don't get fixed, I don't know what will happen. What if the train gets so full, it overflows? Or the engine burns out or just stops running? Or crashes? The Train of Lost Things is broken, and I don't know how to fix it."

16

PLOT TWIST WHEN YOU LEAST EXPECT IT

They pondered that in silence for a few minutes. Then Dina said, "Maybe we can help you out."

Star looked up.

"Right!" Marty said. "I mean, you said the stuff starts flashing when the, um, ghosts are around. We're searching anyway. We can be on the lookout for those at least, right? Would that help a bit?"

"I guess." Star didn't sound too sure, though her face looked more hopeful. Maybe sometimes making a difference wasn't even about doing some huge task to help someone or change their life.

Sometimes it was enough to help them not feel alone.

"There!" said Dina. Across the room, a Raggedy Ann doll pulsed with a faint light. It was nearest to Marty, so he walked over and picked it up. The light flickered in his hands. *On. Off. On. Off.* It was mesmerizing.

Then Star whispered, "There you are," and he looked toward the window. A plump woman with a lined face took shape out of the mist. She was easily as old as Marty's grandma—and yet. And yet, some bit of her still held the air of magic, an inner spark of belief. She was on the other side of the train, and Marty raised his hand to toss the doll to Star, who was closest (and also the most experienced; Marty wasn't sure how he'd feel handing a lost object to an *actual ghost*). In the split second before the doll left his hands, the Echo pop opened up, and he saw the briefest flash of an image: a tiny toddler girl, with chubby cheeks and pillowy arms, clinging to the Raggedy Ann doll that was nearly half her size. He passed the doll into Star's hands, then it was through the train wall and into the arms of the happiest-looking grandma Marty had ever seen. For a second, that spark of magic flared up in her eyes like a real live flame. Then she whirled up toward the stars overhead. And was gone.

"Whoa," said Dina.

What else was there to say?

All of the revelations of the last hour had crowded the jacket out of Marty's mind, just a little. Now, though, it all came back to him in full force. The look on that woman's face when she got her heart's possession back! That—*that*—was the magic he was seeking. The magic he needed.

Pulling out his phone, Marty swiped the screen. The clock said 2:33 A.M. Who knew how long this magical train would let them stay on? A tiny corner of his mind also wondered how he was going to get home, but he pushed that thought away. One worry at a time. Right now: the jacket.

As he dove back into his search, though, he felt a weight in the pit of his stomach. He wanted to help Star with the train, he did. But if they kept getting distracted returning lost stuff, how would they find their own objects? Would they even get to the end of the train? Thankfully, there didn't seem to be any other flashing objects around them. The three searched in silence for a while— hunting, sorting, tossing. They didn't find anything, but they'd gotten near to the end of the car when Dina called his name.

"Over here," she said, with a quiver of excitement in her voice.

Marty shot to her side. There was no jacket anywhere nearby, and he felt his hopes flag.

Then she held out her hand, and he saw something small nestled on her palm. "Didn't you say there were pins on your jacket? Pins with pictures on them?"

Marty took the button from Dina with trembling fingers. It was square, showing a little red car. But what made it special was that it had been wrapped in a very fine black mesh that looked like a tiny window screen. He remembered finding that very pin—showing a car that looked so much like Dad's—and Dad bringing out a scrap of mesh to cover it.

"Remember when you were two or three, and you would sit at the screened window for hours, waiting for me to get home from work?" Dad had said.

Marty had remembered then and he did now, too. He remembered the scratchy bulk of the screen, remembered his own panting anticipation, remembered the rush of raw joy every time he saw Dad's car turn into the driveway.

"As soon as you saw me get out, you'd run shrieking out the door, yelling, 'Daddy, Daddy!' And then you'd jump into my arms."

Marty swallowed a lump in his throat.

"You okay?" Dina asked. "Is it—you know. One of *them*?"

Marty swallowed thickly. "Yeah. It is." He squared his shoulders, stowing the pin safely in his pocket. "This is proof: The jacket's in here somewhere. We've just gotta keep looking. As long as it takes, right? We'll search until we find it."

"Uh," said Star.

Dina and Marty exchanged a worried glance. What now?

"There was something more you started to tell us earlier, but you stopped," Marty said, his mind suddenly racing.

"Right," said Dina. "You said, 'if you find your lost object *in time.*' Then you shut down on us. What is it about time and how long stuff takes? What aren't you telling us?"

Star turned to face them, crossing her skinny arms across her chest. "Kids who find the train get on around midnight, because that's when the train breaks through the fogbank to become visible for that super-short time. But there's a catch. A timeline. The finders always leave at sunrise. The sun comes up and they get pulled right off."

"What?" said Marty. "What are you talking about? Sunrise?"

Dina pulled out her phone and goggled at the screen. "That's in like four hours!"

"Yup," said Star. "Sunrise today is at 7:09 A.M. That's why I said you gotta be good with your time. You don't got much more of it."

"And you're just telling us this *now*?" Dina shrieked.

"I shouldn't be telling you *at all*!" Star snapped back. "That's what the driver said—the kids who get on are supposed to do it all themselves. It's not supposed to be some kind of guided tour. I'm breaking the rules for you here, so stop yelling at me!"

Marty turned the new information over in his mind. Something didn't quite fit. "You said that kids get on at midnight, and they're gone by sunrise. But . . . *you* have been here for ages, you said. How's that even possible?"

"I," said Star, "am a special case."

"And what do you mean by 'pulled off,' anyway? We're like a billion feet up in the sky."

"Train magic," said Star, and pointedly turned away.

It was clear there was quite a bit that she still wasn't telling them. What else was new? Dina was obviously steaming mad, but Marty just wanted to get busy. The clock was counting down, and they'd already wasted enough time in idle wonder.

It was time to stop searching and start finding.

After that, things went both really fast and almost too slowly to be borne. Knowing their deadline gave them a feverish energy that they used to whip through boxes, riffle through bins, and pick through drawers like methodical magpies. They couldn't totally abandon the Lonely Ghosts (the name didn't make sense, but Dina started calling them that, and it stuck), so they developed a quick and efficient system for handling them. Star wasn't very observant, and almost never saw the flashing objects; it was obvious why she hadn't returned many of the lost things. But Marty and Dina were super good at spotting, and as soon as they saw one, they tossed it Star's way. Star did the rest.

They made their way through two more cars in record time. But the farther they got—in spite of the pin in his pocket giving him hope, in spite of the thrill each time a Lonely Ghost recovered a lost object—the more Marty felt his spirits sink. Every passing box, every train car left behind them, was one more place they had not found Marty's jacket or Dina's locket. Every so often Star would say something that should have been reassuring or encouraging. Marty barely listened. And after a while, Star stopped bothering. They all knew how worthless words were.

Marty's jacket and Dina's locket *were* here on the train. But the chances of finding them were looking slimmer and slimmer. They'd almost finished searching the whole train, and all they'd found was one lousy pin.

What if their time ran out and they hadn't found their objects at all? Sunrise would come and they'd have to leave, and that would be that. His one chance to get the jacket back, gone. He thought again of Dad's pale face, his look of hope and love and pride when he'd first given Marty the jacket and explained how it would store their memories. If there was anything that would keep Dad alive, zap his bad cancer cells, and get him back on the road to good health, that jacket was it. Marty *had* to find it. And he would.

In that split second, Marty decided.

Sunrise or not, he'd find a way to stay on. Star had done that. Why couldn't he? He wasn't going to fail Dad.

Marty wasn't leaving this train without the jacket.

Bolstered by his new resolve, Marty marched toward the connector tunnel that led to the next car (only two left till the engine!). Just then, the train gave a shudder. Before Marty could brace himself, there was a violent lurch. It was stronger than usual, and next to him Star grabbed onto a nearby bar. Marty had been mid-step, and he went skidding into the side of the car. The floor tilted and buckled under him. Dina dropped and rolled across the ground like a ball.

The jarring movement stopped, but Marty's breath still came in quick pants. "That was—" he gasped. "Wow."

Star shot toward the door. "That darned engine! I've been out of the cab for too long. I'd better go see what I can do from up front."

"Should we"—started Dina, but the door slammed shut behind Star—"help?" Dina groaned aloud. "How can she even know what to do? Do you ever feel like she's bluffing with all of this? I mean, she's a kid! She can't run the train."

Marty struggled to his feet, stepping over a piece of clothing that lay wadded on the floor. "She's been here a while. I'm sure she's learned stuff. Or maybe the driver taught her before she left?" He frowned and bent over the thing on the ground. It was woolen and orange. But right next to it, something else caught his eye. Could that be . . .

He picked the scarf up slowly, with the small item caught underneath.

"Or maybe the train didn't break until Star took over. Didn't she kind of say that? That it's been getting worse since the driver left? Maybe *Star's* the one breaking it." Dina stayed flopped on the ground, her head in her hands. "I'm so tired of all this. Part of me wants to stay here and search and search forever till I find my locket. The other part is like, *Who am I kidding?* I mean, you've got a chance to find your jacket. It's big, right? It's a proper-sized thing! A jacket! But with this huge old train? And all these mountains of stuff? Like, literal mountains, right? Do you actually think I'm going to find one tiny—"

"Hey!" Marty said. His hands trembled as he held the scarf up.

Dina frowned. "Star's scarf. It must have come off her neck when we all fell."

"No. The scarf was what made me notice, but it had fallen onto something on the ground. Something else. *Look.*" He tugged at the scarf and worked the item loose from its threads, then held his hand out to Dina. Resting on his palm was an ornate silver locket. It looked super old, the silver dull and tarnished. The locket hung on a fine double-linked chain that looked exactly like a railway track.

The locket was in the shape of a train's engine.

Marty would have bet his life on it.

This was Dina's missing locket.

17

A WINDOW ON THE WHOLE WIDE WORLD

Dina froze. Her eyes bulged.

With trembling hands, she untangled the locket the rest of the way from the scarf. She clicked open the latch and spent long seconds staring at it, her eyes as bright as Christmas lights. They actually shimmered, Marty thought with amazement. Then she gave a deep, happy sigh, and looked in his direction.

"It is, isn't it?" he said.

Dina closed her eyes. Then she threw her head back and shrieked, "YESSSS!" She laughed aloud. "Boy, was that a long time coming." Then her voice went soft and she held the necklace out to him. "Do you want to . . . have a look?"

Marty reached one finger out and stroked the etched top. It was warm from Dina's palm as she placed it in his. The panel was open to show a tiny image of a smiling lady with a baby's face held up next to hers. The lady's lips were puckered into a kissy face at the baby's cheek.

As Marty's hand lingered on the silvery surface, the Echo popped up. He watched along with Dina as a youngish, smiling lady—the same one in the tiny photo—held a hand out in front of her. In that hand she held the locket and, as they watched, the lady reached up and fastened it around the neck of a tiny, stick-skinny toddler. The kid couldn't have been more than two or three, but it was unmistakably Dina. Her face showed the same fierce pride and had the identical stubborn chin. Now, though, her look was radiant with love. Her smile ate up her face.

Dina pulled her hand back and the image disappeared.

"Your mom," Marty said quietly. "Wow."

"Yeah," said Dina. Then she sighed. "It's weird seeing her again—after so long."

There was a silence. Then Marty said, "I guess we'd better get back to searching." He frowned. "Well, I guess I need to. Since you, um, found yours."

Dina shook her head. She'd fastened the locket around her

neck and it seemed to put a sort of shine onto her face. Or maybe that was just what happy looked like. "We're in this together. We found my lost thing, now we're gonna find yours."

"What about Star and the engine?"

"We'll make our way to her. There's not many more cars to go, and now that we're not searching for a tiny locket, we can go a lot faster. And we can't help the Lonely Ghosts without Star, anyway. Come on, Marty! Let's do this."

In the end, though they started with mounds of enthusiasm, it was a depressingly short search. Dina was right: It was a *lot* quicker to only be looking for a jacket. Especially a jacket that, car after car, just wasn't there. On the slightly bright side, Marty did find another pin, one that showed a cheeky-looking duck (in honor of one of his and Dad's favorite YouTube songs, the one that started "A duck went down to the lemonade stand," and that Marty could still sing all the way through).

The find should have made Marty feel better, but it actually made him feel worse. He was glad for it, sure. But two pins do not a jacket make, and—truthfully—the more bits of his past he found scattered in nooks and corners, the more he felt himself cracking into tiny pieces. The more his life, all of it, intact as it used to be, started to feel broken beyond repair.

Maybe it was hopeless, what he was trying to do.

By the time a half hour had passed, they'd cleared the final car and moved into the hallway passage leading to the engine. Marty felt his heart pooling down around his sneakers.

He was the best finder of anyone he knew. He always had been. Why now, when so much was at stake, why was this practically the only time he *couldn't* find what he was looking for?

"It's in here somewhere," said Dina stubbornly. "It's got to be. Where else would those pins have come from? We just missed it somehow. We'll go back and start again."

Marty sighed. He was trying to hold on to his hope, but it was *so* hard. The floor wobbled again, though at least it wasn't going all herky-jerky like before. "I guess. We should check on Star first. Make sure she's okay with the engine."

Dina took the lead this time, and Marty wafted dispiritedly behind her. But as he stepped through the heavy door into the engine room, he felt his eyes widen. "Wow!"

The front cab of the train was small, but high-tech fancy. There were two shiny leather swivel seats set in front of a whole countertop jam-packed full of buttons, switches, and knobs. Lights flashed. Doodads hummed. Red blinked and orange purred and green glowed and everything whirled with activity and purpose. It was like an enormous gaming console, but instead of moving little pixel-people across a screen, it took a huge magical train across the sky and around the world.

Whoa.

The whole front of the train was one giant window that wrapped around the edges of the cab and stretched like a bubble up over their heads. Looking out, Marty could see the star-studded night sky on all sides. Far, far below glowed the lights of whatever city they were passing. Dina shuffled toward the right-side window, her eyes wide and wondering.

In one of the swiveling seats sat Star, hunched forward over the panel, her fingers flying across a touch screen. Every few seconds she twisted to one side or another, poking a button or pulling a lever. She did not seem to be having a good time.

Marty sank into the seat next to her. "How's the train doing?"

"You're driving this thing?" Dina asked skeptically, turning to look.

Star snorted. "Not likely! Remember that whole wild-horse-slash-dragon thing?" She rounded her back and lightly knocked her forehead against the front screen. "I've been going over and over the settings. There should be some manual override or something, right? The bucking and spinning stuff is getting worse. It's driving me up a wall. Like the expression but also, you know, in real life." She groaned. "Am I failing? I'm failing. Every sunrise, when the pull comes, I feel like it's better that I'm on the train than off it. So I stay. But sometimes I don't know if that's even true."

The three of them stared glumly out at the night sky, while Star's words hung in the silence.

Then Dina asked, "How *do* you stay on the train, if all the kids who come on board are pulled off with the sunrise? You're a special case, you said. What does that mean? How come you're allowed to stay on?"

Marty perked up. This was important information he would need, if he was going to stick to his new plan.

At first Star looked like she wasn't going to answer. Then she shrugged. "I found out by accident the first time. I passed through the cars pretty quick, since I wasn't really looking for a *thing*, you know? I was glad to be here at all." Marty nodded, and she went on. "Then I found the engine. The driver, she wasn't in here. I didn't talk to her till later. But I found the engine. I sat down, strapped myself in, and was chilling up here, I guess."

Marty pondered this. Would he be bold enough to stumble into the engine of a magical train and strap right in to the driver's seat? Star might be young and kind of quiet, but she had guts.

"I wasn't touching anything, just enjoying the ride. Maybe pretending to be in charge, a little bit." Her eyes took on a wistful, faraway look. "And right then I saw the sunrise through the window. This whole . . . wind tornado, sort of? It blew through the train. A great big vacuumy thing, but cool, and super bright.

I don't know if a wind can even be bright, but this one was. I could feel it tugging at me, like at the core of me—I know, weird, right?—not only my hair and clothes and stuff. But it didn't pull me out, and then it was gone. I didn't think about it much more until after, when I met the driver. She was pretty surprised to see me here, I'll tell you that! She liked to stay out of sight when the kids come on board, let them do their thing on their own. But there I was, still on the train. She kind of took me under her wing after that."

"So then you could just stay on?"

"Not exactly. I mean, every sunrise that same wind tries to yank me off. But as long as I'm sitting in the chair"—she tilted her chin at the driver's seat—"and strapped in, it can't get me."

Marty thought about this. Far away, the distant horizon was starting to put out the very palest of shimmers. It wasn't sunrise, not yet, but Marty could tell it wasn't that far away. He pulled his phone out of his pocket and checked the time. 4:49 A.M. A little over two hours to go.

"The last driver *said* that the right person would come along, that they'd know what to do." Star narrowed her eyes at them suddenly.

"Don't look at us like that," snapped Dina. "*We're* not the driver."

"That's not what I was thinking at all. You're here to get your lost stuff. That's totally different." She perked up. "Speaking of lost stuff, did you . . ."

Apparently she could read the answer clearly in Marty's face, because she spun to face Dina, whose hand moved up to her throat. Dina tugged the locket out from under her shirt and cradled it lovingly.

To both of their surprise, Star leaped out of her seat, releasing the seat belt with a *click*. "Hey! What do you have there?"

Dina took a step back. "It's my locket—my lost thing I came looking for. I found it a few cars back."

"No, wait—that's not your locket. That's *mine*!"

"What are you talking about? It was wedged into some crack on the ground, all—" Dina froze.

Marty finished her thought as he, too, realized. "All tangled up in Star's orange scarf."

Star reached out to grab the necklace from Dina's neck, but Marty jumped in her way. "Wait, Star! It might have been with your scarf, but—I saw the memory. It's Dina's for sure."

At this, Star paused. She looked Dina up and down. Then her eyes widened. She took a step back and collapsed into the driver's seat. "Oh, man," she said. "No way. Oh, man. You'd better look at this."

She turned to a screen in front of the driver's seat. She tapped the screen a few times, pulling up menus and choosing options. She selected a button called History, then clicked on Crew. There was a list of names, with start and end dates. Star selected the last name on the list.

"Here she is," said Star quietly, "the one I was telling you about before. The last driver."

A picture popped up onto the screen. Marty heard a gasp behind him. The image showed the same woman he had seen in the memory from the locket.

The last driver of the Train of Lost Things . . .

. . . was Dina's mother.

18

THE TRICKS FINDERS USE

I had no idea," Star said, shaking her head. The last few minutes had been swallowed up by exclamations of shock and confusion. Marty tried to put himself in Dina's place: She hadn't seen her mother in over six years; now it was like she'd come into a room only to find that the woman had just left by a different door. It didn't seem at all fair.

"Where did she go? And why?" Dina said now, not for the first time.

"She said it was her time to go. But before she left, she gave me that locket. She said—" Star swallowed. "She said I should keep it until the right person came. That I'd know who it was."

"Like she knew I was going to come? But if she did, then she'd have stayed, right? She'd have waited for me."

"Maybe she hoped you would come," said Marty. If there was one thing he knew about parents who loved their children—and those glimpses of the woman with the sad eyes and the gentle hands put her very clearly in that group—it was that they'd never give up a chance like this willingly, not if there was any way around it.

"I think there's only so much time anyone can stay on the train," said Star thoughtfully. "Once enough time passes, the Other Side pulls too hard. Maybe she stayed as long as she could."

Marty thought about that, wondered if that made things better or worse for Dina. If she had gotten here earlier, would she have been able to see her mother, in real life, here on the train? The idea scrambled his brain. He didn't even want to think what it was doing to Dina.

Dina jumped up and started pacing back and forth across the narrow space behind the seats. "I'm not leaving," she said. "I'm going to stay right here on the train. Just stay here forever. This is the last place she was—it's almost like finding her, isn't it? That's what she would have wanted."

Marty and Star exchanged a look. It was uncomfortably close to his own newly decided plan. But now that he was hearing it from Dina, he was suddenly less sure. "Do you really think so?" he asked.

Dina slumped. "I don't know. But I do know that *you* saw her, you spent time with her." She turned a laser gaze on Star. "I want you to tell me *everything* about her."

Marty squinted out the window. The glimmer at the edge of the sky was starting to take itself seriously now, like it knew this was really happening. Sunrise couldn't be far off. Was there still a chance he could find his jacket before the pull came? The girls leaned in close together, Dina firing questions and drinking in the answers, soaking up memories of her mother spongelike. Star was eager to give out what she knew.

But there was too much unfinished for Marty to sit here with them. He would have said as much if they'd asked, but neither looked in his direction.

As he gazed outside, the train listed a bit from one side to the other—not dangerously, not this time. But evidently not fully up and running, either. There was so little time left before sunrise. Even if he tried his best to stay on, there was no guarantee he could manage it. And there was something else, too: The train needed help. Needed fixing.

From the moment he'd first felt the train's headlight gaze

turn on him way back in the clearing, he'd felt a sort of connection (was that too wild?) with the great machine. Now his time was counting down. But Marty was a finder. He hadn't found his jacket. He had the tiniest bit of time left. But what if he spent that time not just looking for the jacket, but also trying to find an actual solution, a way to fix the train for good? It was out there—he knew it; he could just feel it wriggling on the far edges of his mind.

So this was his new plan: He'd find a way to fix the train. And then, in return, the train would let him stay on as long as he needed to find the jacket.

That seemed fair, didn't it?

Pushing open the door, Marty stepped into the hall, then back into the first train car.

Being a good finder took three important qualities: patience, persistence, and imagination. Marty had all of these. Now he put them to use. He moved patiently and steadily through each car, running his eyes across every surface and box and bin: pulling, lifting, checking. A few times he found flashing objects, which he grouped in the center of the car. He tried not to think of their Lonely Ghost owners swirling in the mist outside the window. Hopefully Star would come back in time to help some of them.

Other than that, he moved efficiently along, scouring every bit of each car for the jacket, while also looking carefully for clues to help him solve the mystery of the broken engine.

He did not let himself give up. He persisted, no matter how useless it started to feel: looking through places he'd already looked, recognizing familiar objects he'd seen on the last sweep through. (Finding nothing at all about the broken engine, but how would he know that till he saw it?) It helped a bit that he was tossing things into bins and boxes as he went. Having a tidier space made it easier to see what was out of place. *And* to see what clearly *wasn't* there.

No jacket. No magic train-fixing solution.

He kept on going.

The last quality of a finder was maybe the most important of all. You had to use your imagination, not only looking in all the regular places where you'd expect something to be. After all, if the jacket was where it was supposed to be, he'd have already found it, wouldn't he? "Think outside the box," his mom liked to say on the phone sometimes to her clients, and that's what Marty felt like he was doing now. He ran his hand above the high shelves, scuffed his foot in the narrow gap under the bins, peered into dark crannies and tiny holes that couldn't have held a doll's jacket, much less his own.

And that last spot was where his questing fingers hit something: not cloth, not rough jean fabric, but something else familiar. He scrabbled a bit and pulled it out: a flat, round button with a pin on the back. Marty was almost used to this by now; finding the last two buttons had sent him into a frenzy of searching everything nearby. Now, he knew he had searched every inch of this car. The jacket wasn't in here. So he turned his attention to the pin and looked—really looked—at it. The round button face showed a grinning clown head in front of a striped circus tent. He brought it up closer to his face, soaking in every familiar detail.

A bright pinhole popped out of the center. A button *from his jacket* was popping out an Echo! Marty watched, in wide-eyed astonishment, a scene that was straight from his own past.

They were sitting side by side, Dad and Marty, on a bench inside the darkened tent of a circus. Cartoony music was blaring from loudspeakers, and a super-tall, goofy-looking clown turned cartwheels in the ring in front of them.

Little Marty couldn't have been more than four years old. Watching this now, Marty had a weird double-take feeling: He was older Marty, seeing this chubby little kid on an outing with his dad. But he could also distinctly remember how that tiny kid had felt. Could remember *being* there, in the hot, loud, bustling tent.

He could see all those feelings on his tiny long-ago face: The kid was petrified.

Dad glanced down and saw Marty's expression. "Hey," Dad whispered. "You scared? What's the matter, little guy? Does that clown worry you?"

"Scary clown," Little Marty said, shaking his head.

The clown stopped cartwheeling, and of all things—oh, Marty remembered this so well!—came to stand right in front of their seat. The brightly painted giant unfurled his hand to show a wrapped lollipop. "For you, my man!" boomed the clown. And then he stood there, waiting, hand outstretched.

Marty was paralyzed with fright. He didn't know why he was afraid, except that some of his friends had told him clowns were super scary, and after that he'd never looked at clowns the same way.

Dad brought his brows together like he was thinking. The clown just stood there, waiting. Behind his painted makeup face, his eyes looked kind. And also, maybe, a tiny bit sad.

"How about this?" Dad said. He hoisted Marty up onto his shoulders, grasped him firmly around the legs, then tilted his own head to look up at Marty. He winked. Up that high, Marty felt a thrill of power. He could look down at everyone in the audience, many of whom were staring at him and clapping or laughing. He could look down on the clown, who looked small and actually kind of funny from up here. And he could look down at Dad's face, strong, smiling, and now whispering: "I'll be right here with you. If you want to reach out, you can. I won't let anything happen. I'll always be right here."

Little Marty's chubby hand reached toward the lollipop.

19

ALL THOSE CONNECTIONS ADD UP TO . . . WHAT?

The Echo pop dissolved and Marty was alone in the rocking train car. That lollipop had lasted for the whole afternoon, and he remembered it as one of his top candy experiences ever.

He'd also gone from hating clowns to being obsessed with them, so Mom had to hire two separate clowns for his birthday party that year. Marty smiled to himself. This was a pin to remember! He carefully stashed it in his pocket, alongside the screened car and the duck.

Then he turned and trudged through the connector toward

the next car, turning things over in his mind as he went. That made three pins that he'd found, but the jacket remained stubbornly lost. Obviously, the jacket wasn't hiding from him *deliberately*, but it kind of helped to think of it that way. That it wasn't something Marty was doing wrong, but the scheme of a sneaky object.

Or, perhaps, a sneaky train?

According to Star, the train had its own will and consciousness. He pictured again how the giant headlights had turned to gaze at him back when they'd first gotten to the park. What if it was *the train* keeping the jacket hidden? Could it really do that? And . . . *would* it?

Just like that, every thought Marty had of picking stuff up as he went, of trying to help and fix the train, all of that went jetting right out the window. What had he been thinking? He had to put his own needs first here. He had to think of *Dad*!

The jacket had to be here somewhere. He *would* find it.

He leaped into the new car, his only focus on finding that jacket. Moving in a frenzy, Marty yanked things off shelves. He turned bins upside down. He scrabbled through heap after heap of stuff. By the time he got to the end of the car, his chest was heaving and his breath came in sharp spurts.

Right then the far door opened, framing Dina and Star in the entryway. Their mouths dropped open. Like waking out of a dream, Marty looked back at them from across the swamp of scattered stuff. He had searched his way clear across to the opposite doorway, and now he realized that he could no longer see the floor. The shelves were empty. Every box was overturned. The place looked like it had been through a hurricane, worse even than the last round of the train's loop-de-loop.

"Yikes," said Dina. But she wasn't the one who was going to be left with the mess.

Marty felt suddenly ashamed of himself.

"Are you kidding me?!" said Star.

"I'm sorry!" said Marty, turning around and starting to grab stuff and shovel it into the nearest box. "It's just, the pins, the jacket—it *was* here. But . . . it's not actually *here*." He stopped, a baseball glove in one hand and an anatomically correct frog in the other. He dropped them and reached into his pocket, squeezing the three pins as hard as he could.

"ARGH!" yelled Star, and Dina shook her head in sympathy.

Marty felt tears sting the edges of his eyes. The window outside was distinctly bright now, and Marty knew sunrise couldn't be more than a half hour away. Where was the jacket? Why couldn't he find it? He was squeezing the pins so tight that they made little round dents in his hand. It felt good, having something so real and harsh right there in his grasp. Something he could actually control. For a change.

Dina was still looking at him, but Star scurried around, picking up stuff and straightening boxes. She gave a loud huff of exasperation. "This is going to take me *hours* to sort out," she grumbled. "Thanks a lot! Like it wasn't bad enough in here already."

Marty didn't bother saying that he'd left the first four cars a whole lot better than he'd found them. Because she was right— he'd really messed this one up. But he couldn't entirely regret it. At least he knew for sure the jacket wasn't in this car. There was that, right?

So what happened now?

A soft wind was starting to blow down the center of the car, in the windows, up through the floor.

"Marty," said Dina. "It's almost time."

Well, it had come to that. He knew what he had to do.

"No," said Marty. "It's not time, not for me. I haven't found the jacket, and I'm not ready. I've made my decision." He took a deep breath, saying it out loud for the first time. "I'm not leaving."

Dina frowned, but Star kept huffing around and shoving stuff out of the aisles as though she hadn't heard him. He saw her move right past a couple of flashing items without seeming to see them (or maybe she was just out of sympathy for Lonely Ghosts right now). He hadn't bothered to separate the flashers while he was rampaging, and they winked out here and there from the rubble. As Marty opened his mouth to say something, he saw a blur at the window nearest him. He squinted.

The fog outside that glass was exceptionally thick. And still thickening.

"Star!" he gasped.

The three kids turned toward the window. The mist grew thicker, bulging, and then—it popped clear through the wall *into* the train. A teenager with a pocked face and serious eyes stood in front of them, *inside the train car*, pale and panting slightly.

To their surprise, he looked as solid as any of them.

This was a *ghost*? He'd been mist and fog only seconds before!

"Hey, hey, hey," said Star briskly. "What are you doing in here? Looking for your stuff?"

The boy's lips moved, soundlessly at first, like he was getting the hang of how this whole speaking thing worked. Then he said, "Cheepie."

"Ch—eepie?" said Star.

Marty saw it right away. It was the only thing nearby that was still blinking: a little stuffed bird, pale blue and just bigger than his hand. He picked it up and moved toward the . . . what did he call the boy? Did you count as a ghost if you looked basically solid while traveling inside a speeding Train of Lost Things?

He handed over the bird, his own mind a whirl.

"Thank you!" the boy-ghost breathed. "Oh, thank you! I thought I'd never—"

As Marty stepped back, his hand brushed the boy's. Scratch

"*basically* solid." He couldn't have told that boy's hand from Dina's or Star's.

Now holding his recovered object, the teenager turned and walked in a daze back toward the glass where he'd entered. Never lifting his eyes from the bird, he melted through the wall. There were several seconds where half his body was mist and half was fully alive-looking. Then he was gone, nothing but cloud and memory as he made his way to his final home on the Other Side.

Marty felt his mouth drop open. Inside his brain, gears turned and ends whirred.

There was a spark of an idea churning in his mind. It wasn't fully articulated, but he was onto something. He knew it.

Marty grabbed Star's arm. "I've got a thought," he said. "Come back with me to the engine?"

On his other side, Dina said, "Marty, the sunrise is nearly starting! We can keep looking for your jacket—let's do as much as we can before we get pulled off."

Dina's words tugged at Marty, tugged hard. The sky outside was nearly daylight bright. There was so little time left. What if he couldn't find a way to stay on the train, and this truly *was* his last chance to look for the jacket?

But Star was looking at him now, her eyes eager and curious.

"I've got to do this first," he said to Dina. Then to Star, "Come on. I've got this hunch I want to try out."

. . .

Back in the engine cab, Marty plopped into the conductor's seat while Star settled back in the same chair she'd had earlier. He thought of what Star had said about staying on the train: He snapped the seat belt into place, just in case the sunrise came on fast. Then he turned to study the wide touch screen. "You know how to work this?" he asked her.

"I've played around with it a bit. It's got some kind of a lock setting, though. I can navigate the surface levels, but I think you have to be, like, properly in charge to really get around."

Marty frowned. "Show me what you did earlier. You got a list of the drivers and stuff?"

"Sure," said Star. Her thin fingers flew over the screen, pulling up tabs and clicking boxes. "It's a list of all the drivers and the conductors who've ever run the train."

"And that's why the train's not running right," said Marty, leaning over to study the screen carefully. "It *needs* that. Someone in charge, to keep things organized. That's why it's not working."

"I *am* looking out for the train. I'm doing the best I can. But—"

She didn't need to finish her sentence: It wasn't enough. She was on the train, but she wasn't *part* of it. Not yet, anyway.

"Remember that magical Wi-Fi we were talking about earlier?" Star cocked her head to the side.

"It's out there, the connection. I think we've got to—hook you into it. Connect, right?" Marty selected a tab and zoomed in. "Look at this list of drivers. There should be a place to . . . right here. See this?"

Drivers, the screen said, Add New.

Star's eyes were so wide, they seemed to take up half her face. "The train driver, me? Like, officially? But I'm just . . ."

"A kid?" said Marty. "I don't think it matters. I mean, you've been doing a great job so far. And once you're properly settled in—think about it! You'll be genius." He caught Star's eye. "Yes?"

"Yes!" she squeaked.

Marty pressed lightly on Add New.

Nothing happened. He pressed again, a little more firmly.

"It's grayed out," said Star. "Why is it grayed out?"

Marty went back, then forward again. He touched the button over and over. Nothing. "It's not responding. I wonder why?"

"The train doesn't want me," whispered Star.

"I don't think that's how it works," said Marty. "It's just, for some reason, the link is totally dead." He was quiet for a minute, thinking. He'd been sure this would be enough. Star was the right one for the job. She just needed to be linked into the network. Right?

But there was still something missing.

20

THE ANSWER IS CLEAR AS MIST

Star slumped in place, looking small and lost in the tall leather seat. Outside the window, tendrils of fog licked and crawled like a supernatural trellis vine. Marty blinked.

"Star," he said slowly, "can you tell me again how you came to be on the train?"

She turned to look at him, puzzled. "I told you already. It was that dark, cold night, and I don't like thinking about it, okay?" When he didn't say anything, only kept looking at her expectantly, she gave a low groan. "I guess the truth is I don't remember it all that well. I just remember—being so, so cold." She rubbed her fingers together as though to block out the memory. "I was look-ing for somewhere to stay that was warmer than my box-corner. I climbed up the side of this building. There was supposed to be a spot up on the roof where there was a vent that was warm all night." She frowned, as though some memory was just out of her reach. "I was thinking about being warm, but then I started think-ing about home. How I used to have one, how I wished I had it again. That's when I heard the horn. I was . . . I was climbing this fire-escape ladder up this building, and it was pretty tall. One of my friends down below yelled up at me, but I kept climbing and then—" She stopped speaking, frozen mid-word.

Marty met her eyes. "Did something happen?" he said gently.

Her face had gone chalky. She shook her head.

"Star," Marty whispered. "Can we try something?" When she didn't refuse, he leaned forward and took her hand. It felt bony and birdlike in his. She gripped him back, and together they reached toward the nearest window.

Their clasped hands hit the pane, pushed through it like spoons through Jell-O.

Their hands cleared the window glass easily. Outside was cold, and the buffeting wind yanked and pulled at their fingers. Marty's hand was square, his tan skin dark against the night sky. Star's hand was pale and thin.

"I kept climbing, and I was almost at the roof. Almost there,"

Star whispered. "But just before I grabbed the handle, there was this giant *crack*."

In his grasp, Star's hand shivered.

"The ladder came off the side of the building. It went so fast!"

Her fingers softened in his.

"I fell." She looked straight up and met his gaze. "That's the last thing I remember. I fell. And then, I came to the train."

Through the glass of the window, Marty's hand stood out stark against the licking fog. His fingers were clasped tightly around a hand of cloudy, opaque mist.

He was holding the hand of a ghost.

Star yanked her hand back in the window. She leaped to her feet. "You're kidding me. What the heck is going on here? I'm *dead*? Is that what we're saying? That's what we're saying. If I step outside this train, I'm gonna go all see-through and wisp off to my happy Other Side place and live happily ever after? Or, I guess, *not* or something? Is that what we're saying?"

Marty grabbed her shoulders. "Hey," he said. "Chill! You're not going anywhere. I don't think. I mean, you've been on the train this long, right? Why can't you just stay here?"

Star snorted. "The train doesn't—"

They both turned their heads. A steady beeping came from the console. The last screen was still open and active. DRIVERS, it said. But there was a difference. The second button—ADD NEW—was no longer grayed out.

It flashed a bright, inviting green.

"What just happened?" Star croaked.

"I think you tapped into the Wi-Fi! You needed to know you were—" Marty broke off awkwardly. "Well, you know."

"Dead. I'm dead. Gah!" Swallowing hard, Star reached a hand toward the screen. "You really think I can do this?"

Marty bumped her with his shoulder. "Are you kidding? I've seen you at the controls. And the way you stabilized things earlier? You told that train what to do, and it listened. Even without being linked up. You've totally got this."

Star jutted her chin out and broke into a smile. "I've got this," she whispered.

She pressed the button. Immediately, an avatar image popped up. She barked out a laugh. "Look! That's me! Wait—what kind of horror-shot is that?"

It was a pretty bad picture, Marty thought. Star had pigtails and was missing both her front teeth. Her grin was the exact definition of *cheesy*. He wanted to tell her it wasn't that bad, but he actually had to clap both hands over his mouth to keep from laughing out loud. "Maybe the train will let you . . . update it?" He gasped and choked on a guffaw.

Star glared at him and turned back to the screen.

CONFIRM DRIVER STAR BURTON: YES / NO

Star didn't hesitate.

YES

The whole screen lit up with a warm yellow pulse. Star's name and picture lined up below the one of Dina's mother.

Star spun around to face Marty, all thoughts of bad profile pictures apparently forgotten. "Wow," she said. "Do I look different? 'Cuz I feel different. I feel like I should have some kind of fancy cap to wear. Or a badge or something. Do I get one of those?"

Marty laughed easily this time. "I have no idea. But if there is a driver's cap hanging around here somewhere, I'm sure you'll be the one to find it."

Star tilted her head and reached out to touch the wall. "Do you feel that?"

Marty knew exactly what she meant. It was less something happening and more something *no longer* happening—the wobbly, churning, ship-on-the-ocean wavering they'd felt since stepping onto the train. It had stopped the moment Star had officially become the train's driver.

"You should think about updating your hairstyle to match your avatar, though." Marty couldn't help himself. "I mean, there's a certain classy sort of look to—"

Star elbowed him in the stomach. "I'm in charge here now,"

she said fiercely. "You don't get to bad-mouth my pro-pic. I rocked those tails *and* that gap-tooth grin."

The Train of Lost Things rumbled in agreement.

After establishing her authority to her satisfaction, Star sat back down at the controls and started navigating the new options and communication levels that she now had access to. The huge grin on her face showed how much she was enjoying her new status. The train seemed to be enjoying it, too, if the purr-hum in the background was any indicator. Outside the enormous front window, the first bar of the sunrise stretched a golden finger up the far horizon.

The rush of getting Star settled had wiped everything else from his mind, but it all came crashing back on him now. Marty had done it! He'd fixed the train. It would run smoothly from now on. (It still needed a conductor, he was sure. But at least with a driver in place, it could manage till then.)

Where did that leave Marty? His time was up, and he hadn't found his jacket. He looked down at his tightly fastened seat belt. He could try and stay on, like he'd planned. Would it even work for him like it had for Star? It turned out there was a serious difference between the two of them, what with her being a *ghost* and all. She had been dead all along; that had to put her in a different league.

It made sense, now that he thought about it. You had to be

dead to be a driver—or a conductor, probably—but you also had to be aware of the fact and understand it before you could officially take on the job. Dina's mom must have known this, must have known that Star could be the next driver. But she had waited for Star to discover that in her own time. To discover her own deadness, too. Now Star had done both.

The ache for his lost jacket pulsed again. He knew the jacket was somewhere on the train. He'd found all those pins, after all. He was sure he could find it, if he just had a little more time. Could he *make* some more of that time? If this seat belt trick worked, he could stay on as long as he needed to. As long as it took to find the jacket. But . . .

Marty had to think.

Leaving Star in the engine room clicking links and exploring subfolders, he made his way back through the cars. His mind raced furiously. Say he managed to stay on. He'd have all the time in the world to search. Sooner or later he'd find the jacket. And then what? Marty reached into his pocket and squeezed his hand around the pins he'd found.

He pulled one out and looked at the tiny image, cramped inside his sweaty palm. He wanted the jacket, he needed to have it back—*Dad* needed to have it back.

Or . . . did he?

What if it took days? What if it took a week? How much good

would the jacket do for Dad if it took a bunch of their actual time together for him to find it?

Was Marty willing to become a lost thing himself, even for a while, in order to get his jacket back?

And if he did get the jacket back, then how would he go about leaving the train, exactly, once he'd missed that drop-off window? Could he leap off the side all on his own and, what, plummet down through space? He shuddered. He really didn't think magic worked like that. You couldn't just make up your own rules.

For the first time Marty noticed the narrow light strips that lined the edges of the cars. They seemed to be keeping time with him as he walked through the train: flaring up as he neared, dimming as he passed. Star had hooked right into the main Wi-Fi; she had the boss connection. But Marty? Well, maybe he had his own little hotspot running on the side.

Was that too weird, even for a boy walking down a magical train?

Weird or not, Marty felt the mind of the train, as real as a second person standing next to him, like it was waiting for his decision.

What *would* he decide?

Marty thought again of Dad leaning toward him, eyes bright

as he ran his fingers along the pins on the collar. Was it really the jacket making his eyes shine? Or was it—could have been, all along—*Marty himself* who held the magic?

If, just *if*, Dad did have only days left, was Marty willing to spend even one of them away from his side, chasing his past at the cost of his present?

He couldn't do it.

Marty had no idea how much longer Dad had, but he wasn't going to be away from him one minute more than he needed to. He didn't know if he could help, if anything could help, but there was one thing he *could* do.

He could be there.

"I'm sorry," he whispered, resting a hand lightly on the compartment wall. "I can't stay. I have to go home."

There are some steps that can't be taken, some doors that won't ever open, until the way behind has been thoroughly shut off. Call it magic or miracle or meant to be: The only way to truly move forward is to turn your back on the past.

Marty made his decision. He squared his shoulders with the strength of it. He turned. The train lurched. He stumbled. As he fell, he caught hold of a string, which upset a shelf, which sent a cascade of objects toppling around him.

When he regained his balance, one object was clearly visible at his feet.

It was shaped like an egg. It was a whistle.

Dad's long-lost eggwhistle!

Marty would not be going home empty-handed after all.

21

RIDING THE
WIND-WAVE HOME

Marty found Dina on the roof of the train, looking out toward the sunrise with glistening eyes. She turned toward him as he scrambled up through the hatch and came to stand next to her. He planted his feet wide so he wouldn't wobble, but the train's ride was smooth as a lullaby.

"It's time, isn't it?" Dina said.

Marty nodded, but he didn't need to. They could both see the warm bump of the sun nosing up over the horizon, splashing them all over with newborn light. At the same time, the rushing wind tunnel around the train changed to something else—a warmer breeze, with some kind of perfume to it. A bit like snickerdoodle cookies, actually. It blew a good bit stronger, too. Not a puff of air but the insistent tug of invisible hands. (It reminded Marty of the wind that had blown so hard around the train back when they'd found it in the park, come to think of it.)

He knew they didn't have long.

"You okay?" Marty asked. Not long ago, Dina, too, had been all set to stay on the train. Now, the way she was looking wistfully out at the horizon, Marty could tell her thinking had shifted.

Maybe they'd all been a bit changed by their magical train ride.

"Yeah." Dina scrubbed her fisted hands across her eyes. "I didn't tell you everything, before."

This didn't surprise Marty, but he kept quiet.

"My parents divorced when I was really small." Dina sighed. "My mom was a complicated person. She made my dad believe she didn't love him anymore. But later he found out she was actually super sick, and that's why she sent us away. She didn't want us to see her like that. She thought we'd have a better life without her."

Marty frowned. He didn't like the talk of super-sick parents, but more than anything his heart was wringing for Dina. He almost wanted to reach out and grab her hand (but he had his limits).

"I only found out all this a couple months ago. Dad started

looking for Mom after she hadn't been in touch with him for a bunch of years. My grandma thought she'd ditched us and was off living her carefree life, but my dad said he knew her too well. He figured something had to be up. Even if she didn't love him anymore, he knew how much she loved me. When she first made us go, he wanted to give her some space, respect her wishes and all that. He left her alone for a bit, figured she'd come around. Finally, he started sending letters and emails and making phone calls, doing all that people-searching stuff you can do online." Dina shrugged. "She'd been missing for a while by then. Or, like, missing to us, I guess. And it turned out she wasn't missing. She'd, you know. Gone. Died."

Marty shook his head. All that he should have been saying was jammed up inside his head: *I'm so sorry* and *That's awful* and *How on earth did you go on after you found out she'd died?* Of course, Dina hadn't been living with her mom at the time, hardly knew her anymore, but *still*.

None of the words got out. They stayed there, bottled up behind his voice box, pushing to get out but not ever breaking through.

Dina went on. "At first my dad didn't want to tell me what had happened. He thought it would just make me unhappy, and it's not like I would have known the difference since she wasn't there with us. Why make your kid sad for no reason, right? But then I started asking questions about her, so finally he told me everything." She gave a long sigh. The wind was blowing stronger now, but the suction of the train's roof held them in place so far against the tug of the sunrise. "I don't remember her all that well, and Dad never talks about her much. He isn't a big talker, my dad. And, I mean, she already wasn't with us, you know? So at first, after finding out, I thought nothing had to change at all."

It was strange, Marty thought, how two people could have such an opposite view of something. How to him, the idea of someone being gone forever felt—*was*—huge, insurmountable. Yet Dina seemed to have gone out of her way to keep going on as if nothing had changed. Maybe the truest things in life were those that lay somewhere in between forever and nothing at all. Maybe that's all life really was, when you came down to it.

"So you came looking for the train."

"It's funny—I barely remembered anything about it, not till I lost the locket. Once I found that was gone, I went wild. I *had* to get it back. And then . . . it was like I knew how. Of course! It would be on the Train of Lost Things. I just had to find the train. I didn't remember the actual story at all, not till I saw that memory when I touched the locket. Saw her telling me the story. I guess I'm not surprised she came here to be the driver."

Marty thought about that. "Do you think—I mean, she already

knew she was sick when you left, right? I wonder if maybe—" He couldn't go on.

Dina nodded. "I was thinking the same thing. She came here hoping I might show up sooner or later. She was looking out for me. Then she found my locket and kept it safe for me, too."

"She really loved you," Marty said.

"Yeah. I guess she did."

"What are you going to do now?"

Dina held out the necklace. "Now I've seen her. I've got her right here." She thumped her chest. "Now I'm going back home. I've got my people waiting." She smiled, and in that smile Marty could see it all: the missing, the love for the mother she'd barely known, but twined through all of that, the comfort of the family she had, the assurance of their love. The knowledge of warmth awaiting her, not far away.

This brought something important to mind. "Wait—we've been chugging around all night at crazy speeds. Where even are we?"

Dina rolled her eyes. "Marty. This is a magical train. Don't you think the magic knows what to do?"

As if in agreement, the train roof under them gave a little hiccup.

"Do you ever get the feeling," Marty said, "that this train is . . . maybe even *more* magical than it's letting on?"

Dina laughed, and patted the floor next to her. "All the time," she whispered.

Marty looked down off the side of the train, because the wind was getting stronger now, almost too strong to resist. Away below them, far out but clearly visible, was the grassy field where they'd first hopped on. They'd circled around after all! Beyond the borders of the park were houses, streets, and farther yet the deep city, with apartment buildings and flashing traffic lights and a monorail. He wasn't ready to go, though. Not yet. He grabbed the railing with both hands.

Beside him, Dina flung her arms wide and let out a whoop of laughter. "Don't look like that! We're going to be all right. Don't you see? Everything's going to be okay now."

Marty gave her a weak half smile. "I was thinking. We're both out there, in town, in the real world. I wonder how far we are from each other."

Dina's feet were skidding along the roof now, but she grabbed the rail with one hand and whipped out her phone with the other. "Maybe we're not so far as we think! What's your number?"

Marty shouted it out, right as the wind caught and lifted her. Dina flashed a thumbs-up and yelled, "I'll text you. I promise!"

Then she was gone.

. . .

There was a scuffle and Star's head poked out of the opening hatch. "Marty!" she yelped. "Where's Dina?"

"She's already gone. I'm about to get bounced, too. What are you doing up here?" Marty yelled over the wind. He was gripping the bar with both hands, trying to last as long as he could. But he knew he had seconds left, not minutes. "Don't you have a train to run or something?"

In reply, Star reached the highest rung of the ladder. For a second she paused and her face flashed in a twinge of panic, like a lingering sliver of memory. Then she shook herself, as though throwing off her old life for the last time. She flung her hands up in the air and shrieked with delight. "Look! No hands!"

"You're the driver now," Marty said. "That pull's nothing for you anymore."

He clung tighter to his own spot. Just another moment. He wasn't quite ready to go yet.

"I'll take good care of her," said Star, growing more serious. She flattened a palm against the train's nearest surface, stroked it lovingly. "We'll be okay." And Marty could have sworn he felt a gentle hum ripple below the surface. Kind of like a purr.

"You still need a conductor, though."

"Someone will turn up," Star said. "They always do."

Marty couldn't believe his adventure was over. "You take care of yourself," he said, swallowing.

Star gave a wicked grin. "I always do."

With a nod, Marty felt the wind gear up for its last big burst. He pried his fingers loose from the railing. Catching Star's eye, he tried to shoot out his arm to give her a thumbs-up. Instead, his whole body tipped forward as the wind scooped him up like an airy whirlpool. This time, it didn't bounce him back toward the center. It tossed him up and out.

Marty was windborne . . . he was floating . . . he was part of the sky.

At first he kept his eyes squeezed tightly shut. But not for long. This was the coolest moment of his life; no way was he going to spend it cowering and hiding.

He opened his eyes.

For a quick second, the train's engine loomed up in front of him. The great high beams held his gaze like a huge pair of metal eyes. Then, as the wind started flipping him over, one headlight flickered in a great big magical wink.

Marty's feet toppled over his head. Then he was through the cloud cover and plummeting downward.

He was going home.

22

UNSPOKEN THOUGHTS AND SECRET DREAMS

The sun was all the way up by the time Marty tiptoed in through the back door. To his enormous relief, the house was totally quiet. It was Sunday morning, but still; Mom must have had a really late night to not be up yet. Dad, of course, sometimes didn't wake till nearly noon.

He found the note he'd left still wedged into the back door to the kitchen. He pulled it off, crumpled it into a ball, and threw it in the trash. As he did, he looked out the window above the sink. He squinted into the clear sunny sky.

There was nothing. Not a wisp of cloud nor a curl of fog in sight.

On second thought, Marty pulled the note back out from the top of the trash heap. He smoothed it flat, then folded it and stuck it in his pocket.

It had happened. It really *had*.

Suddenly he shifted in place and flung his hands behind him. His backpack! It wasn't on his back! Then he remembered pulling it off when he'd sat down next to Star in the engine.

Marty had left his backpack on the train.

His eyes widened in panic. How was he going to explain to his mom what had happened to it? More important, he thought, squeezing his hands into fists: How do you go from being the best finder around to being the kind of kid who boards a magical train to find a lost item and not only *doesn't* find it but actually loses something else in the process?

It was too awful to think about. So Marty put that out of his mind. Instead, he closed his right hand around the eggwhistle, safely nestled in one pocket, and his left hand around the pins in the other.

At least he hadn't come back with nothing.

Marty left the kitchen, skirted the stairs, and eased open the door leading into the den. The blinds were pulled down, leaving the room in near darkness. On a far armchair, Mom was curled up with her laptop balanced on the armrest and her legs tucked to her chest. Her mouth was open, her head back. A faint snore came from her throat, each puff of air lifting and ruffling her bangs on her forehead.

Moving with the lightest of tiptoe treads, Marty approached the hospital bed. He stepped around the IV drip and shifted a pill bottle from the bed onto the night table. The bottle rattled faintly and his dad rolled over.

Dad's eyes opened. His gaunt face broke into a smile. "Scooter!"

"Dad!" Marty breathed.

With that, all Marty's other thoughts fell away, unimportant as fluff in the wind.

Dad raised an eyebrow. His breath came in shallow puffs, but his eyes crackled with curiosity. "You've got something—going on, don't you?" He panted a bit. "There's that—look about you. You smell like . . . grand adventure?"

"Don't I, though!"

Dad scooted over to make room next to him on the bed. Marty needed no further encouragement. He gingerly eased himself in next to his dad, moving carefully so as not to bump up against him—he knew how fragile Dad's bones were—but getting as close as he safely could.

And then he began to speak. He started with the jacket and how important it was to him and how he'd felt when he learned it was lost; how he'd left the house to find the Train of Lost Things;

how he'd heard the train's horn calling him across the dark night streets.

At this, Dad's breath caught. His eyes went round as marbles. "You—you found—it?" Dad panted. "The Train of Lost Things?"

"Did I ever," said Marty. He started describing the whole adventure, spending a long time on what the train was like and the rules of being there, how they'd worked to fix it, and how amazing the whole thing was. As he went on, though, he started to stammer a bit.

Because, of course, there was one big thing missing.

"The—jacket," said Dad eagerly. "You—found it?"

And now he had to confess to Dad his deepest and darkest failure: That he'd done all of this, had the most amazing adventure, *found the Train of Lost Things*, but he still, *still*, had not found the precious lost jacket.

The one and only reason he'd gone to begin with.

Once again Marty clutched the smooth, comforting shape of the eggwhistle. "I didn't, Dad. I'm so sorry. I tried my best, but—" He shook his head. He looked up, bracing himself for the disappointment he was sure he'd see on Dad's face.

Instead, Dad was grinning. "That train outsmarted you, huh?"

Marty was so relieved that he laughed out loud. "I guess so. But—I didn't exactly come back empty-handed."

"Oh?" Dad tilted his head to the side.

Marty slowly held his hand out. He spread his fingers so Dad could see what lay in his palm.

The bed next to him started to tremble violently. "Where—did you—get that?"

Marty placed the whistle into Dad's hand, closing his thin fingers around it.

"You—found—it's my—eggwhistle!" Dad's eyes swam with tears. "I can't—believe it. After all—these years!"

"I hardly know how it happened," said Marty. "I searched all over the train for my jacket, Dad. We both did. There was another girl there with me, Dina. And Star." He had so much to tell him that his story was getting as tangled as a headphone cord in a beach bag. But mostly, everything else was pushed away at the awe and shock and delight on Dad's face. In a certain light, he almost looked like a kid again, all glee and satisfaction of his deepest wish coming to life.

"It was on the train all this time," said Dad. He shook his head, a slight, nearly imperceptible movement. "I always did want—to see that train."

Marty looked, *really* looked at his dad's paper-thin face, cheekbones sharp as wings framing his face. His labored breaths, growing shallower by the second and starting up a weird rattle now. His mother's words rang in his ears: *"There's nothing more they can do. . . . At the most, we've got days left."*

Suddenly, Marty knew. Jacket or not, eggwhistle or not: His dad had come to the end of the line. But . . . maybe he didn't have to be all the way gone.

"Tell me—more," said Dad. "I want to hear—all about it."

"Here's the thing, Dad," Marty said. A huge lump rose in his throat.

He couldn't do this.

He *could* do this.

He had to.

"The train's been broken—not running right for a while now. We got it part of the way working. We got a driver set up, and she's got it running smooth again. But the train's not all the way fixed yet." Marty swallowed again.

His dad's hand was squeezing the eggwhistle so tightly that his knuckles were white.

Marty reached out and closed both his hands around his dad's. "I've got an idea, Dad. Kind of a crazy idea. But I think—I think you might like it. First, I need to tell you the rest of the story of the Train of Lost Things."

23

ONE LAST CALL
IN THE NIGHT

They stayed like that for ages, curled in close together. He told Dad all about the train, every bit of their adventure and all they'd done. He told Dad everything he'd kept locked inside him all these last months of sickness, everything he'd been afraid to say: how scared he was of Dad going away, how much he would miss him, how he knew Dad's time was coming soon. And that it was okay with him.

It nearly gutted him, but he said it.

Then Dad started talking, a low buzz of words at first. But it was the first time all day that he'd spoken without the gargling rattle and the constant stops to puff out his breath. He told Marty stories of when he was little. He told him about his dreams for Marty's future. He told him how proud he was of Marty right now. At some point, Marty realized that his mom had woken up and was sitting on the other side of the bed, her arm snaked around Dad's shoulders, her eyes flooded.

They kept on like this until Marty suddenly realized that it had been a while since anyone had said anything. He jerked around to look at his dad. He saw.

Dad's eyes were closed. His face was flat. He was gone.

His hand still clutched the eggwhistle.

Marty buried his face in his hands and sobbed.

It was almost too much to bear, Marty thought later that afternoon. The rest of the day had passed in a blur. Mom was alternating between a sort of stupor and a rush of everything-that-needed-doing.

When someone dies, there are a lot of things that need doing.

Marty pushed it all aside and escaped to his room. His safe zone. But even here he wasn't safe, was he? Right in the middle of his desk sat the star-shaped pin Dad had given him the day before. No matter where he went, he couldn't escape reality, couldn't escape the memories.

Yet . . . Marty realized he didn't want to escape. He picked up the pin and clutched it in his hand, adding it to the three pins he'd brought back from the train. There was no jacket to affix them to. There was no Echo popping up from any of these objects. But that didn't keep the memories away. They would always be there; they were part of him, after all.

Marty closed his eyes and let himself find his own way to the past.

By the time night came, the house had settled a bit. The first wave of relatives wouldn't arrive until the next morning. Two long-faced men in suits had taken his dad's body.

His dad's *body*. How had it come to that?

Unable to sleep, Marty paced back and forth across his room. He had set the pins on the windowsill and he looked at them now, from one to the other to the other. If not for those three he'd brought back . . . no, he couldn't doubt the truth of his adventure. He *knew* it had really happened.

The eggwhistle had stayed with his dad. It would go into his casket.

Dad would have wanted it that way.

Marty rested both hands on the sill and flung the window wide open. He leaned out, tilting back his head and leaning his face to the night sky. The tree outside his window was bare. Sometime in the last few hours, every last leaf had fallen off. It looked dead. But Marty knew it wasn't. Not really.

"I wish . . ."

He didn't get any farther. Because right then, a sound cut the night in two. A single sound: just one. It wasn't repeated, but that sound would echo in Marty's mind long over the decades to come, reliving the moment when he heard, just above his house, the sound of the long, low horn of a train.

And after it, so faint you might almost have missed it if you weren't listening with every cell in your body, the sharp trill of a whistle.

The sort of call made by a conductor, hanging off the back of a train.

A conductor blowing on an eggwhistle.

EPILOGUE

M arty was at dinner when he heard the doorbell ring. Ten days had passed since he'd said goodbye to his dad for the last time. Ten days that felt like forever and yet seemed to pass in a single eye's blink.

For the first time, the house was quiet again, and empty.

So empty.

The last of the relatives had gone home. The hospice people had cleared out the medical equipment from the den.

Nobody went in the den now. Not ever.

Marty and his mom sat at the kitchen counter, picking at

wontons and fried noodles. Into the silence came a zinging sound: the buzz of a phone on silent mode (*Fake-silent*, Marty always thought—why did they say silent when it was so not?). Frowning, Marty squinted at the screen. He didn't recognize the number, but the message made him sit up fast.

Hey! Marty? Finally got up the nerve to text. Tell me all that really happened!

With a half laugh, half sob, Marty tapped a reply. It was Dina!

its me. hv been thinking same thing

So if I'm texting you and you're texting back, then . . .

We should get ice cream sometime

yeah

Meet at the park tomorrow
after school?

For the first time since he'd been home, Marty felt his whole body relax into a smile. It didn't last, though. Because the second he put his phone down, reality came rushing back to him. The train really *had* happened (he hadn't doubted it, honestly, but it felt good to have proof).

That didn't actually change anything.

His dad was still gone. And he was still the kid who had gone all the way into the sky on a magical train, and had managed to fail at what he set out to do. Whatever good spin he tried to put on it, those were the facts. That was the thing about being a finder: There was no halfway win. You either found what you were looking for, or you didn't.

That was when the doorbell rang.

Lifting his head, Marty looked at his mom's slumped shoulders. They weren't expecting anybody to come over, but these days you never knew. People dropped by all the time, for no particular reason, and then you had to smile and nod and make small talk when all you wanted to do was be alone with the quiet.

Alone to think. Alone to remember.

His mom evidently felt the same, because she didn't move a muscle. Or maybe she didn't hear the bell; she looked like her mind was miles away.

Marty almost decided to ignore it, too. But the ring came again, and it had a certain *something*. He couldn't have said what, but whatever it was hoisted him off the stool, across the floor, down the hall.

He flung open the front door.

There was no one there.

Marty blinked at the empty landing outside, and only then did he notice a square box resting on the top step, right in front of the door. A curling tendril of fog licked up and over its surface.

The mail? At this hour?

It didn't seem likely, but there was the box, and . . . that was his name scrawled on it in black marker: *Marty Torphil*.

Puzzled, Marty tucked the package under his arm and shut the door behind him.

For no reason he could explain, he didn't go back into the kitchen, but carried the box up to his room. He put it in the center of his bed, then sat down facing it, tucking his legs crosswise in front of him.

He took a deep breath.

The flaps were tucked under each other to keep it shut. There was no tape.

There was no address.

Just Marty's name shouting out from the top.

Marty picked up the box. "Heavier than a boiled egg," he whispered, his heart in his throat. "Lighter than a laptop." He shook it. Nothing . . .

No, *something*.

A slight shifting, and a faint scratch, like something hard brushing the edges of the box.

Throwing ritual aside, Marty tore open the flaps.

Into his lap fell the jacket.

His jacket. The very one he'd lost.

He laid it out on the bed, pushing the box off the edge so the jacket's sleeves could lie flat. He ran his hands lightly over each of the pins, the badges, and the sewn-on patch. They were all there—all except the three missing ones. He grabbed those from his windowsill, the screen and the duck and the circus clown (and the new star, too). He pinned each of them into place.

He found a special place for the star, right in the front.

And then, from inside the box, something rattled.

He tilted the box and tipped it over. A single pin fell out onto the floor.

Marty picked it up, and immediately he frowned. He didn't recognize this at all; it wasn't one of his pins.

Then what was it?

He moved under the lamp so he could study the image in careful detail. As he did, his eyes widened.

The oval pin was the length of his index finger, and the backdrop gleamed silver in the light. The image showed a long, winding train, sleek as a bullet, and next to it, a tall conductor, smiling into the night.

The conductor was wearing a black backpack with tiny purple zipper pulls.

Marty's fingers trembled as he moved the pin to the collar of the jacket and pinned it in place. Tears filled his eyes. He could hear the words in his mind, as clear as if Dad were standing in the room next to him. *"Stick it on anywhere you like, Scooter."*

Marty smiled and spoke aloud the words Dad had said to him so long ago: "That's how you capture today and keep it forever."

Marty put his arms into the jacket.

He did up the buttons and went downstairs. His mom was still slumped at the kitchen counter, her untouched noodles congealing in their pool of sauce in her bowl. He came up behind her and put one hand on her shoulder.

Mom looked up, bleary-eyed. She frowned at him. "Where did you—hey! Isn't that the jacket you lost?"

Marty smiled (a bit damply, true, but it was a real smile). "Mom. Have I got some stuff to tell you!"

Late at night, that's when the magic was strongest. When stories swirled like fog and trembled like dreams made real. When heartbreak and tears and hugs made the world a little better than it was before.

That was tonight.

Tomorrow there would be ice cream with a new friend.

And after that? Living. Something he wanted to start doing a lot more of. He thought Jax might just understand if Marty told him the whole story. Might want to give their friendship another try.

Yeah, there was a whole lot of living ahead. New memories to make.

Marty stuffed his hands into his jacket pocket and started his story.

ACKNOWLEDGMENTS

I suppose I have the Paris airport security to thank for this book. Several years ago, we experienced a family vacation trip that was essentially one long string of disasters. (It makes for a fascinating story, but unfortunately, the combined sum of events would be far too unrealistic for fiction!) As the last straw on this debacle of a trip, my teen daughter's jean jacket—with its long-standing and lovingly collected pins and badges—disappeared after our trip through security. Coming as it did on the tail of everything else, it just felt like one thing too much.

But it also got me thinking: about lost things, how precious they can be, how powerless we are when they go astray. I've always felt that pull for things I've lost, to where I think back on certain objects years later, and always with that gut pang of longing. Standing in my office that day, feeling bad for my daughter, was when the first story seed idea came my way.

What if there *was* a way to reclaim those lost things? *What if . . . ?*

The second factor that contributed to this book was my

mother's battle with lung cancer: brief, fierce, and fatal. This amazing woman lived just four months after her out-of-the-blue diagnosis, before passing away in 2003. Her death was the catalyst that first pushed me to take my writing seriously, but not until now have I felt up to probing the experience of losing her. Of course, this is not her story, nor is it mine. But it is a story that comes from my heart, and as such, I hope that wherever she is, she knows that I am thinking of her. That she has never lost a moment of my heart's time.

I have so many others to thank for their role in bringing this book to life: Jill Santopolo, Talia Benamy, Michael Green, and the whole Philomel team. Erin Murphy, Dennis Stephens, and the EMLA gang. My amazing clients, who are so patient when I am slower than I ought to be. Jaime Zollars and Theresa Evangelista for gorgeous cover artistry. Julie Berry, Debbie Kovacs, Natalie Lorenzi, Julie Phillipps, Nancy Werlin, and Kip Wilson for being A+ critique partners. Sarah Azibo and Kirsten Cappy for all you do. And last but not least, to my family: Zack, Lauren, and most especially, Kim—your jacket is gone but not forgotten.

Ammi-Joan Paquette has spent much of her life with her nose in a book—whether reading or writing. She is the author of several books for young readers, including the Princess Juniper series, *Two Truths and a Lie*, *Nowhere Girl*, *Rules for Ghosting*, and *The Tiptoe Guide to Tracking Fairies*. She lives near Boston with her husband and two daughters.

You can visit Ammi-Joan Paquette at ajpaquette.com
and follow her on Twitter @joanpaq